FREEDOM

by

D.W. Lewis

The Caerwyn Chronicles

Book II

ISBN: 9781972803028
Renaissance Hands Books
2nd Edition
© 2026 David Lewis
All Rights Reserved

A note from out author

Caerwyn Chronicles is a look at a family line as they go from one generation to the next through history. The family is not a powerful family, or a particularly wealthy family, they are normal people living ordinary lives. They are affected by the politics going on around them. The family is also met with different religious beliefs and finally are introduced to Christianity. This book takes a realistic look at the issues of the time, including slavery and the attitudes of the people about those issues.

Content advisory: This work contains depictions of enslavement, coercion, and historical violence that may be distressing for some readers.

This story is written in solidarity with those whose dignity and humanity persisted despite systems that sought to deny them both.

Part I

Yearning For Freedom
(68 AD)

Chapter 1

Aedan walked through the busy streets of Londinium, the air was thick with the smell of humanity. He had been here many times before with his parents, but this was his first time coming alone. He wasn't totally alone, Rian, the slave from the inn was with him. Rian preferred to stay with the wagon and the mules, so Aedan was practically on his own. He was there to buy supplies needed for the family run caupona; most of their guests were Roman or Roman supporters who wanted Roman food.

The columns that formed the front of the marketplace towered over Aedan as he walked past. The courtyard that he walked into was busier than the streets if that were possible. There were people dressed in Romani fashions and people dressed in the old way, true Briton fashion. Of course, there was a constant reminder of who was in power, the legionaries who marched through the market.

The food stalls that sold Romani food were all in a certain section of the market. Aedan hated the path over there because he needed to walk past the slave market. It was a small section of the market, but visible. The Romans liked to remind people that they could control their lives even more if they didn't behave. Aedan made it a point to avert his eyes ever since he was a child. The humiliation the people went through was more than he liked to see.

As he was walking past, something caught his eye. There was a flash of color he didn't expect and he turned without thinking. On the platform was a girl with hair the color of glowing embers. He had never seen anything like that before. She had a strong jawline and a short nose. She was standing on the platform, trying to cover herself. They had just removed her tunic, and she stood there wearing only a loincloth. She wasn't crying or complaining, she glared at all the men there as if daring one to come too close.

Aedan remembered his mother's stories of experiencing a similar humiliation when she was sold as a slave. His temper flared, he stepped into the throng of people at the market he could hear some of the men saying crude things he would not dare repeat. They were talking about that girl with ember-colored hair. Aedan felt the anger inside of him rising. The man on the platform raised his hand for silence.

"This young barbarian comes from the far north, beyond the northern border. She would be a good addition to your household." The men started to talk again, more comments that disturbed Aedan. "We can start with eight hundred sestertii," the man continued.

"Here," said one of the men. Aedan did not like the way he looked at the girl. He looked at his purse and thought about the two thousand sestertii he had scraped together for this trip. It represented three months of caring for guests, three months of hard work for his parents, himself and his brother and sister. Aedan did most of the calculations for the inn, he knew what the money was worth.

"Is there an increase on eight hundred?" the man on the platform was saying. Aedan raised his hand without thinking. "Ah the young man wants her, perhaps he needs companionship." That comment brought jeers and laughter from the other men. Aedan was sick that anyone would think that of him. The decision to bid had been impulsive compared to the way Aedan normally acted. Another bid was made and he was ready to quit. He had no logical reason to save this girl. Slavery was part of life and what happened to the slaves was none of his business.

Aedon sighed and turned to leave. He couldn't responsibly spend any money on this. It was a foolish idea to bid, what if he had won? He would be responsible for a slave and not have enough to buy the supplies needed. As he walked off, he thought about his sister. This girl was about her age; his sister was worth more than two thousand sestertii. Without giving it another thought he turned and bid one thousand!

"He's desperate for companionship," the slave trader called out amidst a round of laughter. "What do you say men?" There was another round of laughter and men calling out obscene suggestions. Another man bid and Aedan decided that maybe the gods had saved him from his own rash actions. He didn't need to be responsible for a slave; he had enough to take care of. As the oldest of three children, he was expected to take care of his siblings and help run the family inn. Aedan turned away again and started to head to the stalls he needed to visit.

"Young man," the slave trader called, trying to increase the bid. "Look at her, such beauty, you can't just walk away, cay you?" This was met by more laughter and jeers. Aedan felt the blood rush to his face and turned back to face the man. She was beautiful, her hair and angular jaw made her unlike any woman he had ever seen. She was thin, they had not fed her enough, but he could tell she would have a fine figure if she were treated well. If he had met her in the village he would want to know more about her.

"One thousand, four hundred!" Aedan heard himself saying. He didn't know what compelled him, he just knew that this poor girl deserved better.

"Sold!" the man threw the girl's tunic at her, and she rapidly put it back on.

Aedan slowly walked to the platform and counted out the coins The man roughly pushed the girl to him and laughed. Aedan grabbed the girl's hand gently and led her away from the laughter.

At first the girl resisted, and Aedan wasn't sure why. Then he realized, if she was from the north she likely had not learned any Latin. She was likely Caledonian, Aedan had heard of them but never met one.

"Come with me," Aedan said in his own tongue. It was different from the tongue of the Caledonians, but he knew they were similar enough to communicate. He prayed to the gods that she would understand. She seemed to understand but shook her head. Aedan put his arm around her and whispered that these men wanted to hurt her and he wouldn't allow it. She finally went with him.

When they got to the wagon Rian looked at Aedan and the girl. Rian was in his late forties and hated just about everyone. This oldest son of his master did have some redeeming qualities; he had taken after his mother in appearance and intelligence. His father Corin Lupinus was a big and powerful man, while Aedon was average size and strength. His dark hair was straight, and he always kept it clean and combed. He also kept his jaw clean shaven, although he likely wasn't old enough to grow a beard.

"What is this?" Rian asked.

"I bought this girl," Aedan said. "It was a quick decision that will likely get me into trouble." Rian laughed, he turned to the girl and asked her in the Caledonian tongue what her name was.

"Maeli," the girl said softly. Aedan looked at Rian in disbelief. He had never asked the man where he had come from, he just knew he was from the north.

"Maeli," Rian said, "where are you from?"

"Coire Mór" the girl replied. Rian nodded, he knew the place, it was obvious that his young master did not.

"She's from the far north, the islands," Rian said. "She's a Caledonian."

"What am I to do?" Aedan said. "It took almost all my money to get her away from them." Rian smiled again.

"It seems our young master feels he has made a mistake," Rian said to Maeli. Maeli looked lost, "he's spent the money he was to use for food to give to the slavers. You are beautiful, I can see why he would do that." Maeli just glared at the men while Aedan found himself blushing. She was beautiful, her red hair was tangled but still stood out. She had a softly curving jaw and eyes the color of the sea.

Aedan told Rian and Maeli to get into the wagon, he would have to go home empty handed. They had enough supplies for a few more days; he prayed to the gods that a wealthy visitor would come that he could charge extra. He had done that before, his mother didn't like it, but his father approved. The trip home would take a day, and he could try to think of a way to tell his parents what he had done.

Chapter 2

Aedan had a plan! He told Rian to drive the wagon up to a familiar domus just outside of Londinium. He stepped down and told Rian to stay and watch the girl. He slowly walked to the entrance, hoping he would find a warm reception and the help he needed. He knocked on the door and a young slave girl answered.

"Is your Domina in?" Aedon asked the girl. She nodded and rushed off to get her mistress. Aedon waited nervously at the entrance until a familiar voice came from the atrium.

"Aedon?" the voice called to him, and soon he saw Druscilla Flavia walking out to greet him. "It is you! What a surprise!" Druscilla hugged the young man and then held him at arm's length to look at him. "You've grown again."

"I doubt it," Aedon said with a smile, "I don't think I will be as tall as my father."

"Good," Druscilla said conspiratorially, "your father is too tall! I don't see how your mother can stand cricking her neck to talk to him." Druscilla took the boy by the hand and pulled him down to the atrium where she made him sit and then told the girl to bring wine. Druscilla had been in the room the night Aedan was born. In those days she had been hiding from people that wanted to prevent her marriage to her now husband, Titus

Septimius Marcellus. Titus now served as secretary to the Roman governor in Britannia.

To Aedan, Druscilla was like an aunt, he had fond memories of her from when he was a young boy. She often visited the inn to send reports back to her father. He hoped now that she would be willing to help him. After some wine and catching up on family Aedan decided to broach the problem he had before him.

"I've created some trouble for myself," Aedan finally said, looking down into his wine goblet. Druscilla let out a short laugh, she couldn't imagine this fastidious young man getting into trouble. The gods had not given her any children, and she accepted that so long as she had Aedan and his siblings.

"What could you have possibly done?" Druscilla asked.

"I spent all the money I needed for supplies,' Aedan admitted.

"What did you spend it on?" Druscilla asked, shaking her head.

"A slave," Aedan said softly. Druscilla's eyebrows went up. "The men at the market were saying terrible things. I couldn't stop myself. She's about the same age as mother was when she was taken. I just don't know what to do." Druscilla stood up and walked to where the young man was sitting. She could see he was at a loss for what to do.

"Let me meet this girl," Druscilla said, "I have a need for a new slave. If she fits my needs, I will buy her from you." Aedan let out a sigh of relief. This would save him from getting into trouble. The two stood and walked out to the wagon where Rian was sitting watch over Maeli. Maeli was glaring at the ground with an expression that Aedan was starting to think was permanent.

"Oh my," Druscilla said, "she's beautiful, and that hair! She will fit into our household beautifully. What did you pay for her."

"One thousand four hundred sestertii," Aedan said softly. Druscilla let out a snort.

"They took advantage of you," Druscilla said with a grin. "No matter, I can afford that." Druscilla took Aedan back into the house and left him in the atrium while she counted out the money. When she returned with the purse, she handed it over and called for her head slave. An old man with grey hair and a slightly hunched back came out.

"Josephus," Druscilla said, "please go with Aedan and get the expensive slave from him." Josephus didn't fully understand what she was talking about but went out with Aedan to the wagon. Josephus greeted Maeli in the Caledonian tongue, much to the surprise of everyone.

"Come with me," Josephus said, "I will take you to your new home." Maeli looked from the old man to Aedan.

"He sold me?" the girl seemed livid.

"Hush girl," Rian scolded. Maeli glared from Rian to Aedas. Aedas felt a little shame for selling her. He had swooped in as if it was great rescue and then profited off her. He wished he had another choice, but he needed the funds to buy supplies.

As he watched the red hair disappear into the domus he couldn't help but wonder if he did the right thing. The best thing would have been to walk on and leave her fate to the gods. Maybe he was right in saving her, Druscilla was a good Domina, she rarely beat her slaves.

The market felt quiet now, as Aedan was lost in his own thoughts. In his mind's eye he could see her standing defiantly on that platform, glaring at anyone who dared to bid. He could hear her anger at the idea that he had sold her. Why would that bother her? He wondered about that too. Did she think of him as a hero only to be rejected by him?

Aedan bought the supplies as quickly as he could. He was now a day behind schedule and would need to spend the night in town. His parents usually would go to Druscilla for the night, but he was afraid to run into the girl again. He had enough money left for a room at a caupona, so that's where he would stay. He slept fitfully that night and took the new supplies home the next day.

When he arrived home, he was greeted by his parents, Corin Lupinus and Eira Ennia. They had been born in Brittania, sold into slavery to Roma and then returned as citizens of Roma. A citizenship they passed on to him, his brother Cador and sister Seren. His mother had been worried that he was a day late, but his father seemed to understand.

"A young man needs his freedom," his father had said to his mother the night before as she stayed up listening for his return. Aedan gave them his apology for being late, but no explanation. He had no idea how to explain the trip to his parents. As the supplies were unloaded, Aedan was sent to the kitchen for food.

Seren was three years younger than Aedan and idolized her elder brother. She cut him some bread and cheese and put it on a platter for him. She then poured him a tankard of ale before sitting down with him.

"So?" Seren said, "why were you late?"

"It's complicated," Aedas said, drinking his ale.

"Was it a girl?" Seren asked with a knowing smile.

"No!" Aedan exclaimed, "I'm betrothed." Aedan had been officially betrothed a few months back. His father had made arrangements with the chief of Caedwyn for Aedan to marry his oldest, Caela. She was a year younger than Aedan, and very beautiful. It was a good match, and Aedan had been grateful to his father.

"Ugh!" Seren said, "Caela is so full of herself. You deserve someone better. She's so dull!" Aedan let out a laugh, Caela was difficult to talk to, her favorite subject was her beauty. He ate some of his food and then looked around.

"To be honest," Aedan said conspiratorially, "I did meet a girl, she has hair the color of a glowing ember." Seren gave her an unbelieving look. "It was beautiful."

"Where did you meet this girl?" Seren asked with a smile. Aedan loved his sister's smile; it always lit up her face. Seren looked very different from the family. She had hair the color of straw and eyes as blue as the sky.

"She's a new slave in the Marcellus domus," Aedan said. Seren let out a loud laugh and Aedan put his hands out to quiet her. "Don't tell anyone. She hates me anyway, so I don't want to talk anymore about it."

"She hates you already?" Seren asked, her eyebrows raising "what do you do to her?"

"Nothing bad," Aedan replied, "I don't want to talk about it."

"I'm sure we will be visiting Amita Druscilla soon enough," Seren said with a sly smile. Aedan glared at her, the threat unspoken, Seren hopped up from her bench and rushed off to help with the daily tasks. Aedan sighed and finished his food before getting up and helping.

As he carried supplies from the courtyard to the storage room he thought again about Maeli. He couldn't help but wonder what she might say to Seren if asked about him.

Chapter 3

Druscilla insisted that all working in her household were clean and well dressed. Maeli was taken to a small room at the far end of the domus where she was given opportunity to bathe and then given a clean tunic and under tunic, she was also handed a brown cloak and sandals. After getting cleaned up she was brought to Josephus for inspection.

Josephus nodded his approval and then told the girl to join him in the kitchen. They sat at a table and Josephus gave her a bowl of potage. The first real food she had seen in a long time and she ate hungrily. After she finished her second bowl, she sat back in her chair.

"You were hungry," Josephus said with a smile.

"They didn't feed us much," Maeli said with a scowl.

"Can I ask how you got here?" Josephus asked carefully.

"Last season my village was attacked by another village," Maeli started, "I was not killed because the chief wanted me for his son. I refused to marry him, I fought him. I stopped eating, I hit anyone that came close. I didn't give them a chance. After almost a full season they were tired of me and the chief sold me to the iron men. They brought me here to sell and that boy," she said this word with disdain "who sold me to this place. I am not a pig to be bought and sold!"

"I agree, none of us are swine" Josephus said, "that boy is the son of two slaves, people who used to work in Domina Druscilla's house. They were given freedom, and I think that boy hoped the same for you." Maeli shook her head; she wasn't going to forgive easily. Just because he thought he was doing something nice, he still treated her like an object. To be taken as a slave was accepted as a tragic part of life. To be displayed like an object to be sold was humiliating.

The boy who bought her had been handsome; she hoped he saw her for what she was. She had a fleeting hope that he would give her liberty. Instead, he saw her as property and sold her. He was no better than the iron men.

Josephus took Maeli to Domina Druscilla who suggested Maeli be made her new attendant. She would help Druscilla dress, do her hair and fetch things around the domus. She would also go out with her and help with anything she needed. This was all explained to her by Josephus as Maeli did not speak Latin. After showing her the responsibilities, Josephus left.

Maeli felt abandoned and alone. The lady she was to call "Domina" looked at her from where she was reclining. Finally, the lady stood up and walked over to her. Maeli had no idea how she was to communicate with this woman; she didn't know her tongue.

"So, you are Maeli," the lady said in the tongue of the Britons. Maeli was stunned; she could understand that tongue. Her jaw dropped and Druscilla laughed. "Surprised I know your tongue?"

"It isn't my tongue," Maeli said softly.

"Oh," Druscilla said, "it's close. If all you people could agree on one language my life would be easier." Maeli just looked at the ground at Druscilla's feet. "Oh, darling child," Druscilla said, "you mustn't let me upset you."

"You don't upset me," Maeli said. Druscilla went back to her reclinium and lay back down.

"Your name," Druscilla said thoughtfully, "in private we will keep it, in public I will call you Maelia. As will my husband." Maeli nodded her head ever so slightly.

Her mother had given her the name because her hair looked like fire. She had been proud of her hair as a child. It was what had saved her as that chief found it to be impressive. Maybe that is what got that boy that just sold her to pay attention as well, there were not many people here with hair like hers.

"Maeli," Druscilla was taking again, Maeli looked up. "If you can find the kitchen, tell them I am ready for my meal. I think we should go out afterwards to show you the land we own." Maeli nodded and walked off in the direction she thought was right.

The domus was a big place, they had been in the atrium, a room with a small opening to the sky. Off in a far corner was a corridor that Josephus had shown her. He said only slaves used it. She knew to follow it to the end and then turn and follow that to the end to find the kitchen.

The room was small and smelled of smoke and spices. There were various meats and bunches of herbs hanging from the ceiling. At a low counter a woman was preparing some sort of meat dish. Maeli went to her and got her attention.

"Domina says she wants her meal," Maeli said.

"You're the new girl?" the cook asked,

"Yes," Maeli said, "I'm Maeli."

"I'm Emerita," said the cook. "You find Nessa and she will help you prepare for the meal." Maeli went back down the corridor peeking in at every door. Each room was more unusual than the last. One had three beds around a low table; another had different looking beds scattered around and plants hanging in pots. She also found a full pond inside the domus! She chuckled to herself as she wondered if there were any fish in the pond. Finally in the room she had used to clean up she found the girl who had helped her earlier.

"Nessa," Maeli said, "how do I prepare for Domina's meal?"

"She usually eats in the oecus when the Domine is away," Nessa said. "We will take some dishes there and Emerita will bring the food." Nessa led her to a storage room filled with platters, bowls, cups and goblets. She showed her how to select some and took her to another room that had more of those small beds.

"Go and tell Domina Druscilla to come to the oecus," Nessa said. Maeli walked back down the corridor to the atrium where Druscilla was reclining and humming a tune. Before interrupting, Maeli listened to the tune. It was beautiful, she liked to sing some of the old songs her father had taught her and enjoyed listening to music again.

"Domina?" Maeli said softly, "your meal is ready in the oecus." Druscilla stood up and smiled at Maeli. Without another word she started to walk through the atrium to another entrance. Maeli stood still, unsure where to go. Druscilla stopped and looked at her.

"You follow me," Druscilla said softly, "just keep a step or two behind or the others will get upset." Maeli walked behind Druscilla through a different corridor. This one was wider and had colorful stones on the floor that made a beautiful pattern.

Nessa was waiting with food like Maeli had never seen before. There were strange looking meats covered with spices and sauces she didn't recognize. As she stood there watching Nessa put food into dishes for Druscilla, she felt herself starting to lose her balance. She had not had a full night's sleep in a while and was feeling the exhaustion from the journey catching up with her.

"She looks so tired," Maeli heard Domina Druscilla say. "Take her to bed, I can care for myself this evening. Go, take care of her." Maeli felt herself being pulled by the arm down a corridor and into a small room. There was a straw mat on the floor with a big woolen covering.

Nessa helped her remove her cloak and tunic before easing her onto the mat. The cover on the bed was scratchy and warm. As Maeli heard Nessa leaving the room, flashes of her old life came to her memory. The warmth from the fire. Her sister snuggled up next to her. Her father telling stories of the ancestors. For the first time in weeks, Maeli let herself cry.

Chapter 4

"A Senator!" Selena whispered to Aedan as he came down the stairs. He had heard the commotion from his room as the horses and chariots rode into the courtyard. They had never had a Senator from Roma in their inn. He rushed to join his father to greet their important visitor.

"Senator," Corin said as Aedan walked up, "this is my son Marcus, he will be responsible for making sure you have everything you need for your stay." Aedan did not like his Roman name 'Marcus' but it helped make the Romani feel at home. "Son, this is Senator Marcus Fabius Severus." Aedan greeted the Senator formally before looking around the courtyard.

There were two chariots, horses, legionaries and slaves to care for. He excused himself and got to work helping organize everything. He called for Rian to help get the horses to the stable and help the chariot drivers move the chariots into the stable. The Senator's luggage was put into the biggest room close to the baths while the other officials were given other rooms. The legionaries were given mats to sleep in the courtyard, close to the fire for warmth.

Corin watched his son proudly as he sat to listen to the Senator talk about his visit to Britannia. He was talking about investments he needed to visit, Corin was half listening but enjoyed watching his children work. Aedon and Seren both took after their mother, organized and good hosts. His middle son Cador was like him, tall and strong but not very good around people. Cador helped with carrying luggage and moving the chariots but left everything else to his brother and sister.

It took a good hour to get everything organized and into its place. The Senator talked the whole time, most of it was just nonsense. Finally, the Senator said something that made Corin pay attention.

"I will be meeting with some generals tomorrow," the Senator said, "also the governor of Brittania will be here. I'm told his secretary is part owner of this caupona."

"Yes, Domine Senator," Corin said, "we are co-owners. He inherited most of it when his wife's father passed, we were given a small share as well."

"Very good," the Senator said, he seemed distracted now. "I see you have a good bath house; I will now go and take my bath before we eat." Corin was relieved to see the Senator rush off, yelling for a slave to come and help him. Aedan came over and sat with his father.

"We will have a crowd here tomorrow," Corin said to Aedan, "get your mother and Hilarus, discuss what food is needed, then go into town to buy what we don't have in the storeroom." Hilarus was the old cook that came with this inn when it was bought by Druscilla's father. At this point he directed the meal preparation as their other slave Elen did most of the actual work. Seren and Eira also enjoyed helping prepare meals and would be needed for the upcoming feast.

After a long talk discussing a menu with Hilarus, his mother and one of the Senator's aides, Aedan was ready to go with a list of ingredients needed and a purse of coins. He decided to take the back roads to Caerwyn instead of the one built by the Romans. It was a more scenic route, have him a moment to breathe. The morning had been long and taxing.

Further up the path he saw the distinct figure of his younger brother. He was talking to someone that Aedan didn't recognize. As he got closer Cador turned to him and looked startled. The man he was talking with was older and had severe scarring on his face. Like he had been burned. Aedan saw Cador hand something to the man before the man rushed off into the woods.

"Who was that?" Aedan asked as he got closer.

"Promise you won't tell?" Cador said quietly.

"I suppose," Aedan was very curious now.

"He's a poacher," Cador admitted. The land here was under Roman control and hunting was very limited. Many men hunted illegally and sold the meat to people or kept it for their own families. Aedan had bought meat from poachers in desperate times as well. Anything for their guests.

"What did he say he could get?" Aedan asked.

"He said there are deer," Cador said, "I heard we are to have a feast and a deer would give us meat."

"Did I see you give him money?" Aedan asked.

"A little now, the rest later," Cador said. Aedan shook his head, it was bad business, they wouldn't see that man again. However, his brother was still young and needed to learn for himself.

"We will keep that as a surprise," Aedan said, he didn't want his brother embarrassed when the man didn't bring any deer meat. "I'm going to the market; can you make sure there is enough feed in the stable for all the horses?" Cador nodded and walked back in the direction of the inn.

Aedan continued to the Caerwyn market. It was very different from the one in Londinium, there were a few small stalls run by farmers, a butcher and a fishmonger. There were no specialty foods for Romans and no slave markets here. It had only been a month since visiting the Londinium market, so their supply of specialty food would be enough for the time the Senator was there. He would likely have to visit again shortly after this feast, but he would have the money from the Senator. He was already calculating the charge for the Senator in his head. He was always reasonable with money, but a big event like this always brought extra for the family.

After making the purchases needed, Aedan returned home using the Roman road. He had to admit it was faster and more convenient. The inn was still busy with all the extra people there. His mother and sister were baking extra bread and Hilarus was sending Elen back and forth to the storeroom for supplies.

The Senator had brought a reclinium from his room to the courtyard and was reclining in the afternoon sun and dictating some sort of official statement to his scribe. Aedan saw his father reclining nearby, taking up his role as host. Aedan chuckled to himself, he felt sorry for his father as he knew this was not something he enjoyed. It was expected, though, that the host be nearby in case he was needed. Aedan saw Cador nearby, standing close to his father. Aedan went over to see what was needed.

"How are the supplies in the stable?" Aedan asked Cador. Cador startled, he had been focused on the Senator.

"Fine," Cador said quickly. He turned back to the Senator. Cador had always had an interest in political matters; he was obviously fascinated with what the Senator was doing. Aedan decided to let his brother be, it was good he was learning.

Aedan went back to the kitchen to check everything there. The food had been delivered and Hilarus was happy with all he had. Aedan secretly hoped they could add the deer meat to the menu. Hilarus was always happy to add things to his menu if supplies arrived late. As it was, the deer never arrived, and Aedan was not surprised.

Chapter 5

Maeli looked through the trunk again. She knew what the Domina would want for this journey and wanted to ensure it was all there. She had expected to hate life here, but so far it had been tolerable. She was still a slave and not able to go where she liked, but Druscilla lived an interesting life. Maeli was allowed to be a part of it, even if it was a step behind everyone.

She had started to understand some of the Latin used in the house. She found herself wanting to learn just to be able to follow the conversations. Druscilla was popular among the Romani women living in Londinium, and there were often visitors in the atrium. Druscilla had lived in Britannia for so long she was like a native and could answer just about any question asked about how to survive among barbarians.

Now they were packing to spend a few days at a friend's villa in a village called Caerwyn. Maeli was determined to pack everything right, since this was her first time doing it on her own. After she double checked everything, she let Josephus know the trunk was ready to go into the wagon. Maeli was going to ride with the luggage and not in the fancy wagon, but she was one of the few slaves invited.

As they rode off, the sun in her eyes and wind blowing hard, Maeli found herself smiling. Druscilla had told her to smile when working, and she tried, but this was a real smile. Could she actually be happy? It didn't feel right to be truly happy; she was still alone in the world. Her family was gone, but her mother would be glad she was in the care of Druscilla. Maybe it was good she had been sold by that chief.

"You look happy," said Afer, who was Titus' attendant. Afer was an interesting man, his skin was impossibly dark. He says his parents were captured in a place called Numidia and he had been Titus' attendant from the time Titus was a child.

"I might be," Maeli said, "we're getting out of Londinium." Afer let out a loud laugh.

"I'm glad to see it," Afer said, "you always have a sour face." Maeli couldn't help but laugh at herself. She remembered her mother once telling her something similar. Her father used to tell her that if looks were as deadly as a spear, she would have killed many people.

The two settled in for a long ride, occasionally Afer would point out sights that were of interest to him. Every time they stopped the two would have to climb out and make sure their Domine and Domina had everything they needed. Maeli had not had this much time alone since arriving and was enjoying herself. The day flew by and by evening they were pulling into a domus standing in a field.

They went into a big atrium that seemed to go on forever. There were slaves waiting to help them carry the baggage into the villa. There were also the people that lived in this villa. Maeli was surprised to find they were a Briton man and his wife. They had accepted the Romani way of life and become wealthy trading with them.

Maeli helped Druscilla change and bathe before coming out to eat. Many of the local farmers had been invited over to speak with the governor's secretary. Druscilla reclined in the back of the room with Maeli standing behind her. With everyone speaking the Briton tongue, Maeli could follow the conversations with ease. Everyone had requests for help with various problems they were facing.

Maeli wondered how Domine Titus could stand just sitting and listening to people complain. It was late by the time they were done for the day, and Druscilla could get ready for bed. After Domina was in bed, Maeli was shown to the slaves' quarters. It was colder than Titus' domus, and Maeli huddled up and finally got some sleep.

The next morning Maeli helped Druscilla prepare for a big feast. The whole household was excited because the feast was to welcome someone important from Roma. He was called a Senator, but Maeli understood that he was like a chief. Druscilla had asked for her nicest clothes, which included draping a long piece of cloth around her. After she was done, Druscilla looked so elegant. Maeli was also given a tunic with a purple edging and a gold clasp for her cloak to let everyone know she was an important slave. She felt elegant as well.

They all rode in the official wagon with comfortable seats. They came to a caupona with a sign that had an old symbol, a triskelion, three turns that represented land, people and ancestors. She was a little upset that the Romas took it as a symbol for their inn. Titus and Druscilla entered, Titus held up his arm and Druscilla put her hand on it. It looked like he was presenting her. Afer and Maeli walked a step behind.

The courtyard was filled with people dressed in similar robes. There were Romani warriors all over as well which made Maeli a little nervous. They took a place at the table, Maeli standing behind Druscilla as she reclined. She looked around the group and saw him! The man that sold her to Druscilla.

He was sitting on a bench at the far end of the courtyard between two women. One was about the same age as Maeli and the other was a little older. The woman her age looked at her and her expression changed. She turned to the man and whispered to him, pointing at her. He looked up and his face fell. Obviously, he had told this woman about selling her. He stood up and walked directly towards them.

"Druscilla Flavia," the man said, "how are you?"

"I'm doing well," Druscilla said, "you remember Maelia." Druscilla turned and beckoned Maeli forward. Maeli could feel her face getting red. She wanted to hide but had to step forward.

"Yes Domina?" Maeli asked.

"I know you've met before," Druscilla said, "but you haven't been formally introduced. This is Aedan Marcus Lupinus. His family and I own this caupona together." Maeli gave a polite nod and then stepped backward to her spot. Aedan then beckoned to the older woman who had been sitting next to him. She stepped forward, she was beautiful with dark hair and brown eyes. She was wearing a white tunic with gold trim and a red cloak. When she stood next to Aedan he put his hand on her arm.

"This is Caela," Aedan said to Druscilla, "my betrothed." Maeli felt all the air go out of her. He was betrothed. Of course he was, he was old enough. Why did it surprise her? Druscilla graciously greeted Caela and the couple returned to their seats.

The food came out, and looked and smelled so good. Maeli knew that she would be fed in a few hours. She had been told the slaves would get a special meal as well as the speeches were going on. Afer told her that it was a political event and speeches could take hours. The slaves were to be ready if needed but weren't really supposed to listen to the political secrets of Roma.

After everyone had eaten, they were preparing for the speeches and the slaves were dismissed. As Maeli was sent out of the courtyard, she saw Aedan sitting and laughing with his betrothed. It bothered her, but she didn't really know why. She tried to forget it as she sat down to eat some of the foods that had been left from the feast.

It was supposed to be a treat, but Maeli wished she could have roast boar. Even a bowl of potage would be better than this. It was too rich, too many flavors blended together. Maeli finally found some roast boar and ate it. She left rest to those that would appreciate it.

She asked Afer if she would be allowed to visit the horses in the stable. He told her he would let her know if she was needed. She rushed off to the stable where the horses were enjoying their own feast. She walked over to the horses stood by one of them, slowly petting its neck.

She thought about Aedan, she didn't want to but she couldn't get him out of her mind. She had thought she would never see him again, it made sense that Domina Druscilla and he knew each other. Her initial reaction to hearing he was betrothed was to be upset but she didn't know why.

She remembered thought back to that day in the market. She had just been forced to walk for days and then she was humiliated in front of those laughing men. They seemed to enjoy looking at her, even though she was thin and any curves she had were gone. Then the man that she was sold to gently led her away.

She could remember his warm hand on her shoulder. He was holding her as if her were protecting her from the men. She felt protected by him. Then he betrayed her. She ran her hands down the strong neck of the horse and sighed.

He hadn't really betrayed her. He didn't even know her. He had been a decent person, that was all. He had seen her humiliated and felt like he should do something about it. Her father would have done the same. Maeli sat down on a beam running across the stall she was in and looked the horse in the face. Its eyes looked sad. It wasn't free either.

"You poor thing," Maeli said to the horse, "I bet you would be happier running in a field somewhere."

"He would miss the barley," a male voice behind her made her jump. She turned around and saw Aedan standing close to her.

"I'm sorry," she stammered, "I know I'm not supposed to be here." Maeli stood and turned to return to the slave's quarters.

"You are fine," Aedan said, "the horses aren't complaining." Aedan stepped towards the horse Maeli had been petting and patted its hindquarters. "I'm sure he would be happier running in a field. Unfortunately, he was born in a stable and not a field."

"Are you saying that his being captive is because he was born to it?" Maeli asked. "That doesn't seem right."

"You are right," Aedan nodded, "unfortunately not much in the world is right." Maeli rubbed the back of the horse again, thinking about that.

"Aren't you supposed to be in with the speeches?" Maeli asked.

"It's all Roman politics," Aedan said. "They are having trouble with the emperor; he's like the head chief. I don't understand any of it." Aedan walked around checking to make sure the other horses were all fed. As he walked through, he kept glancing at Maeli. She joined him, enjoying looking at the different horses.

One horse looked like she wasn't standing comfortably. Aedan looked and realized she had kicked all the straw away and was standing on a hard stone surface. He noticed a small sheath of straw laying behind Maeli.

"Can you hand me that straw?" Aedan asked. Maeli nodded and bent down to get the straw. When she handed it to Aedan their hands touched for a moment. Maeli felt a warm feeling go through her body when they touched. She pulled her hand back and saw that Aedan had a strange look on his face. Did he feel something too? Aedan spread the straw out for the horse to have a better surface and turned to face Maeli.

They were very close; Maeli could feel the warmth of his breath. She wanted to step back but found that she couldn't. It was Aedan who finally took a step back. He looked into her eyes, and then her lips. They were slim and cracked from the dry air. They were so inviting.

"I should get back to Caela," Aedan said quickly before rushing past Maeli to the exit to the stables. Maeli sat on a stool and put her head in her hands. What was she thinking?

She had found Aedan charming and liked how he cared for the horses. He was handsome, his smile seemed to make her heart melt. He was betrothed and she was a slave; she had no right to think of him as anything other than her Domina's friend.

Chapter 6

As the final group left the feast, Aedan was ready to collapse. The Senator and all his people retired to the bathhouse, so Aedan went to the tablinum, a small room off the kitchen where they kept their money and record keeping. Cador was sitting at a table with some parchment; he was writing something down. Aedan had never known his brother to do much writing.

Aedan was curious but also needed to write down his figures while they were still in his head. He took out the wax tablet where he kept the daily tallies for the bill. He spent some time scratching the figures onto the tablet. Today was very profitable for the inn. Finally, he looked at Cador who was finishing his writing. Cador rolled his parchment up and put it in his cloak.

"What are you working on?" Aedan asked.

"Making some notes from today," Cador said "it was interesting what the Senator said." Aedan had to admit he hadn't really been paying attention. Sitting between Seren and Caela had been distracting. Seren with her quick wit was making it hard to not to laugh, which is why he had gone to the stable.

"I missed some of it," Aedan admitted.

"The emperor is corrupt," Cador said, "and they want to get the military to back a new emperor."

"That really won't change anything for us," Aedan said.

"It might," Cador said. "With the government in turmoil we might be able to change some things here."

"You sound like a separatist," Aedan said with a chuckle.

"What if I do?" Cador asked, "we are forgetting the old ways as we let the Romans walk all over us."

"I don't know that we are forgetting the old ways," Aedan said, "we still know the stories of our ancestors. We are adapting to new ways."

"Not our ways," Cador said harshly. Aedan wasn't sure how to respond to that. Cador was right that they had adapted to the Roman way of life. There were still many roundhouses out there, but people were starting to build Romam styled homes. Londinium looked more like a Roman town than a Britannic village.

"Maybe you are right," Aedan said, "you need to be careful though. Talking against Rome is treason. Don't let our guest hear you." Cador stood up, he towered over his elder brother.

"I'll be careful," Cador said. He put a hand on Aedan's shoulder as he walked past. "Don't

worry about my brother, I know what I'm doing."
Aedan watched his brother go and couldn't help
but worry.

Aedan walked out to the kitchen where
Seren was organizing the cleaning of the kitchen.
He picked up some of the bowls that had been
recently cleaned and placed them on the shelf
where they were stored.

"Seren?" Aedan started, "have you noticed
anything suspicious about Cador?" Seren put down
the wooden platter she was scraping clean.

"Suspicious?" Seren asked, "not really. He's
always been strange." Aedan laughed and put an
arm around his sister.

"You're right," Aedan said, "but he's never
been stupid. I shouldn't worry about him. I'm just
tired. You get to bed soon; the sun will come
quickly." Seren punched her brother lightly in the
stomach and grinned at him.

"I got enough sleep during those speeches,"
Seren said before returning to her work. Aedan
helped her finish up before the two went to bed.

The sun did come quickly, and Aedan was
still tired when word came that the Senator was
ready to leave. Aedan quickly dressed and went to
his father to tell him what the final charge for the
stay and feast would be. His father insisted that
Aedan join him in speaking with the Senator.

"Domine Senator," Corin said to the Senator, "my son has your ratio for the stay." The Senator beckoned one of his attendants.

"This is my dispensator, Demetrius," the Senator said, "Demetrius, go with the boy and settle my account." Aedan led the dispensator to the kitchen, where he pulled out the wax tablet.

"If you look at this," Aedan said, "the final ratio comes to 68 denarii." Demetrius took a careful look at the tablet. He was a trusted slave, but a slave all the same. Any mistake would lead to punishment.

"One hundred and fifty asses for the wine?" Demetrius asked. "I don't think the wine was that high a quality." Aedan smiled, it was the job of the dispensator to haggle the prices. Aedan's mother had handled this before he had come

to age, and he had fond memories of watching her act offended at such suggestions. Aedan learned that her tactics didn't work for him and used other tactics.

"There was a lot of wine," Aedan said, "I don't believe the Domine Senator went without for his entire stay." Demetrius gave a soft chuckle, obviously he thought that the Senator drank too much. Of course, he wouldn't admit it but having it subtlety mentioned made him more laid back.

"I see," Demetrius said, "are you charging for the legionaries? They slept in the courtyard."

"They slept on our beds and burned our wood," Aedan retorted.

"But they offered their protection of your caupona," Demetrius countered. Now it was Aedan's turn to laugh.

"Fair," Aedan said, "I will remove the charge for the legionaries." He had added a few extra charges, expecting the Senator to haggle the cost. He scratched out the cost of the legionaries on the tablet and changed the final calculation.

Demetrius agreed on this final ratio and counted out the coins. Aedan put the coins in a purse, and they returned to the Senator.

"Your man drives a hard bargain," Aedan said to the Senator. Demetrius gave Aedan a quick smile and then returned to his place. The Senators entourage finally left the courtyard through the big arch that led to the road. As they left, Aedan felt a big load off his shoulders. Corin turned to his son with a questioning look.

"He had 100 asses removed from the cost," Aedan said with a smile.

"You are just like your mother," Corin said with a laugh. The two men walked around to check for any damages while Eira organized the cleaning. As they got to the stables, Aedan thought back to his time with Maeli. He had thought about kissing her.

"Da, do you remember when you and Ma were betrothed?" Aedan asked.

"Of course, son," Corin answered. He found a few tools that were out of place and picked them up to put them away.

"Did you love her at first?" Aedan took a broom and started sweeping some straw back into a stall. Corin laughed,

"I couldn't stand her!" Corin said. "Love came later. Your Ma and I went through a lot together before we were married." Aedan had heard all the stories, they had been captured and enslaved in the city of Roma. They had fallen in love on the journey to Roma.

"I'm not sure I'm in love with Caela," Aedan said. "I don't think we will have the same type of experience."

"I hope not," Corin said with a frown, "we made certain you would be given Roman citizenship and have rights. As for love, I'm sure it will come after you are married, maybe before. You are both still young." It was at least four years before they could marry. Aedan sat on a stool and sighed.

"What if I am in love with another?" Aedan asked. Corin pulled up a stool next to his son and sat.

"That could be a problem," Corin admitted, "are you in love with someone?" Aedan put his head in his hands.

"I don't know," Aedan admitted. "I almost kissed a girl here in the stable during the speeches. I wanted to."

"That would have been improper," Corin said, putting a hand on his son's shoulder. He understood the impulse, but as a good father he had to teach his son what is proper. "Who was it?"

"Maeli," Aedan said softly, Corin gave his son a blank stare. He had no idea who Maeli was. "She's Druscilla's attendant." Aedan still had never told his parents about his rash decision to rescue her from the slave market. As far as his parents were concerned, the girl was a stranger to him.

"With the bright hair?" Corin asked.

"Yes," Aedan said. He smiled at the thought of her hair. It was how Seren had recognized her and pointed her out to him at the feast. Corin saw the smile and realized his son did have feelings for her.

"What do think you should do?" Corin asked. Aedan looked up at the sky coming through the opening in the roof.

"I don't know," Aedan said, "you picked a wonderful woman for me. I appreciate it, Caela is beautiful and a good person. I just don't enjoy spending time with her."

"Have you spent much time with this other girl?" Corin asked.

"Not really," Aedan said.

"Then how can you know it is love and not just that she is something new and exciting?" Corin asked. Aedan stood and walked over to a beam in the stable that he noticed was not sitting right. He adjusted it a little, but the peg that had held it in place was broken.

"We will need to get Rian to fix this," Aedan said. "I'm not sure what I'm feeling," he finally admitted. Corin joined him at the beam and looked at the damage.

"If you decide that you want to break the betrothal," Coin said solemnly, "we can. It would come at great cost, so make sure you really want to do it."

"Thank you Da," Aedan said. He went to find Rian, his mind still going to that red hair.

Chapter 7

Maeli lay on her bed staring at the ceiling. She had not slept well since getting back from Caerwyn a week back. Her mind kept going back to the conversation in the stable. Aedan had seemed so nice, not the monster she had imagined. All the people that knew him spoke well of him. Maeli rolled over and noticed that Josephus and Afer were still awake. They were sitting at the table and talking softly in the light of a small lamp.

Maeli got up and wrapped herself in her cloak before walking to the table. Josephus looked up when she walked over and smiled at her.

"Hello," Josephus said, "still not sleeping?"

"I think she has someone on her mind," Afer said.

"Please join us," Josephus said, pointing to a stool. As Maeli sat, she could see that he was holding a scroll with some strange markings on it. It was strange to see a scroll in the slaves' quarters; they usually cost a lot of money.

"What is this?" Maeli asked, pointing to the scroll.

"It was a gift from one of the Senators slaves," Josephus explained, "he was given it in Roma but has passed it to me."

"But what is it?" Maeli asked. Druscilla had been teaching her to read some Latin, but these markings looked different. She couldn't make sense of them.

"It is a letter," Josephus said, "from another follower of the Mashiach." Maeli had heard about this god, Josephus told her he only had one God named the Mashiach. Josephus had seen him and heard him speak. Maeli had never heard of anyone that met a god.

"I can't read it," Maeli said trying again to make out the letters.

"It's lingua graeca," Josephus said, "the language of the Greacian people. It is a common tongue in my country."

"How many ways of talking are there?" Maeli asked.

"I don't know," Josephus said, "the Torah speaks of a time when God muddled the tongues of the people so they could not become powerful."

"What does this letter say?" Maeli asked, leaning forward.

"It is explaining how the Mashiach has made it possible for everyone to enter the kingdom of God." Josephus said. "Afer and I have been going over it these last few nights."

"Don't let me stop you," Maeli said. She thought that maybe hearing about other things would get her mind off Aedan and she could get some sleep. Josephus started to read, translating from the graeca.

"We boast in our suffering, because it brings stamina, and stamina brings character, and character brings hope," Josephus read.

"That means that we should be happy with suffering?" Afer asked.

"I think it means that when we suffer, we grow as people," Josephus explained. Maeli shook her head. She knew that the gods brought suffering, but she didn't think it could be a good thing. As the men continued to read, Maeli was half listening. She was thinking about her own family story.

Her ancestors had survived harsh winters and had learned from them. Her father had told her stories of her ancestors moving from the hills to the lowlands to escape harsh weather. She supposed she could be thankful that their suffering had taught them to find better places to build. They also improved their building skills to make the houses warmer. Maeli stood up to return to her bed.

"You've had enough?" Josephus said with a smile.

"I'm tired," Maeli said, putting her hand on Josephus' hand. "You've given me something to think about."

"This man Paulos was smart," Josephus said. "Emperor Nero had him executed for what he taught," Josephus added sadly. Maeli walked to her bed. She knew who Nero was, she had sat in meetings with Druscilla where the ladies discussed him. If Nero didn't like these teachings, then she wanted to learn more. She also knew Druscilla was as loyal to the emperor and decided it was best to keep this conversation to herself. Before long she was sleeping soundly.

The next day as Maeli was helping Druscilla dress, Druscilla pointed to a package wrapped in linen on the table. Druscilla asked her to fetch it, when Maeli did, she opened it and pulled out a new cloak. It was a deep green woolen cloak. It didn't have any of the embellishments of Druscilla's other cloaks, but Maeli admired it.

"This is for you," Druscilla said. Maeli couldn't comprehend what she was saying. "I wanted to give you this, try it on." Druscilla held it out and Maeli took the cloak, wrapping it around her shoulders. Druscilla pulled out a bronze clasp with a green bead and helped Maeli fasten it.

"Thank you," Maeli said looking down at it.

"I knew green would be your color!" Druscilla exclaimed. "Now you look like a proper attendant. As Maeli looked at the cloak Druscilla put a hand on her chin and lifted her head so she could look into her eye. "Child," Druscilla said, "as you know I have no children. I have lost three in childbirth and can't stand trying again. I hope that any child I might have had would be like you.

Strong and beautiful." Druscilla dropped her hand and turned her head.

"I've come to like you too Domina," Maeli said. She could hear Druscilla sniff and then she turned back.

"Very good!" Druscilla exclaimed, "let's show off your new cloak. We shall go to town and get some sweet breads." Druscilla walked quickly away and Maeli followed. They walked through the atrium and a few of the slaves noticed her cloak, she could see them whispering. She felt like she was very important.

As they got to the streets, Maeli noticed something wasn't quite right. It was still busy but there were more legionnaires marching around than normal. The people all felt tense as well. She could sense that Druscilla had noticed as well. They walked to a taberna close to the domus to buy something to eat.

When they arrived, there was a group of people milling around the entrance. As the people saw Druscilla a few broke off from the group and came to her.

"Is it true?" one of them asked. Others chimed in with similar questions.

"Is what true?" Druscilla asked.

"Is the governor really dead?" someone else asked.

"I have not heard anything like that," Druscilla said sternly, "I'm certain it is a rumor and nothing more." She didn't seem as certain to Maeli; there had to be a reason for the increased presence from the legion. Druscilla calmly bought some bread and led Maeli away from the shop.

"Come," Druscilla said once they were out of earshot, "we need to get to the forum. Titus is there today." Druscilla walked swiftly through the streets; Maeli had to rush to keep up.

The forum was a large building with a big courtyard. There was a covered corridor with tall columns that surrounded the courtyard on three sides with the official buildings on the fourth side. It was always teeming with people, and Maeli had to stay close to Druscilla. They walked through the corridor, past orators, shrines to the Roman gods and men arguing over some point of the law or another. Finally, they reached the office where Titus took care of legal issues in Londinium. As they entered, Titus was speaking with a man in the armor of a general. He saw Druscilla and quickly went to her.

"You've heard?" Titus said quickly.

"It's true?" Druscilla responded, "the governor has been killed."

"Worse," Titus replied, "Senator Marcus Fabius was killed." Druscilla gasped and took Titus' hand. "And that's not the worst part; he was staying at Caupona Caureni." Druscilla acted as if she was going to faint. Maeli caught her and put her in a chair. Maeli was a little unsure of what was being said, she thought she had heard the name Caupona Caureni before.

"Why was he there?" Druscilla asked, her face pale.

"He had visited a few other places to speak and wanted a few days rest before going on the long journey home," Titus explained. Maeli realized what the Caupona Caureni was, it was Aedan's inn.

Chapter 8

The Senator was back for a few more nights, and Aedan was sure it would only benefit the inn. They would have a reputation as the place Senators come for rest. Aedan was in the courtyard with the Legionaries, helping them build a fire. He laughed when the Senator's dispensator mentioned that they could collect their own wood. Aedan suggested the inn could give their protectors some firewood.

As the fire started to leap high, Aedan saw Cador heading across the courtyard to the arch that led to the road. Aedan got up and rushed to the arch and caught Cador before he got outside.

"Cador," Aedan said, "how are the grain supplies? The Senator expects the best for his horses."

"I will get some more tomorrow," Cador said. Aedan thought he looked distracted and decided it would be good to remind him the next day. Aedan thought about the responsibilities he was given at Cador's age, there was a year between them, but Aedan ran the inn while Cador helped with the stable. He wondered if Cador resented not being given more responsibility, he certainly never acted like he wanted it.

"Great!" Aedan said as cheerfully as he could. "I appreciate all the help; the Senator has made a lot of demands." Cador nodded sternly and stepped towards the arch.

"I'm going for a walk," Cador said. Aedan put his hand on his brother's shoulder, a little annoyed that he had to reach up so far to do so. Cador shrugged his hand off and left quickly. Aedan wasn't sure what was bothering him, sometimes his brother just got into a mood.

Aedan decided to spend some time putting today's figures onto a wax tablet before he forgot them. He sat at the table in the tablinum and scratched the figures into the wax. He thought about his brother's mood. Ever since that poacher had taken his money, he had become more sullen, if that were possible.

Aedan wondered if they could find that poacher and bring him before a magistrate. Cador had used his own money to pay him, which Aedan appreciated, but it meant that he might feel the loss a little more. He decided that he would discuss the matter with his father.

It was late, Aedan went up the stairs to the family quarters. In the large room he shared with his siblings there were three beds, a table and stools. Seren was sitting on one of the stools, mending a tear in one of her tunics. Aedan wished her a good night and got into his bed. He was exhausted and fell asleep quickly.

A loud noise brought Aedan back from a deep sleep. He sat up, the lamp was out and he could see movement in Seren's bed. Cador's bed was still empty.

"What was that?" Seren asked.

"I'm not sure," Aedan said. He stood up and walked to his parents' door, planning to ask if they heard anything. The door flew open and his father stepped out, a sword in his hand. There was another crash from outside and they could hear voices.

"Grab your sword," was all Corin said and he rushed to the stairs. Aedan rushed to his chest by his bed. Inside was the sword his father had given him a year ago. He had never really used it. Aedan rushed to the stairs and as he came down could hear more voices crying out in alarm.

Aedan crept through the kitchen into the courtyard to see the legionaries were moving about and fighting. He couldn't figure out who they were fighting. He could see his father, ever the warrior, rushing into the fight. Aedan wasn't certain what he should do. The people the Romani were fighting with seemed to be normal townspeople. He could see some of them were using farm tools instead of weapons.

It was at that moment that Aedan saw that the door to the Senator's room was swinging open. It looked broken. Aedan stayed close to the wall, trying to avoid the fight to get to the Senator's room. As he got to the door, he looked inside but couldn't see anything.

"Senator?" Aedan called out. He heard some muffled cries. Aedan stepped through the door, his sword straight in front of him. From inside he sensed movement and stepped towards it, something hit his sword and he dropped it immediately. He then heard the Senator cry out. Aedan turned to where the cries came from but still couldn't see anything.

Alone and unarmed, Aedan tried to step back out of the doorway. A large hand grabbed his wrist and pulled him back into the room. Aedan tried to wrench himself free, but the hand was too strong. He remembered something he had seen his sister do as a toddler. When his mother had tried to get her to go somewhere she would just fall. Aedan fell. The hand let go.

Laying on the floor, Aedan felt foolish for letting himself get into this situation. He could hear people moving all around him but could do nothing. He got up on all fours and started to crawl for the door. He moved his hand and felt a sharp pain. He had brushed up against something sharp. He pulled his hand back and could feel the blood running down his finger. He suddenly realized he had found his sword!

Reaching carefully, Aedan found the hilt of his sword and forced himself to stand up. This time he held his sword close, ready to thrust the sword like his father had shown him. Someone brushed against him and he tried to thrust the sword but missed. Aedan took a step backward and into the doorway. He decided to use his body to block the exit until he knew where the Senator was.

"Senator!" Aedan called out again. The answer came as a clear cry for help. Aedan wasn't sure the best move. He could step forward and try to free the Senator, or he could continue with his current plan. Neither seemed smart. Then he had a smart idea. He turned and cried out for help. He heard his father's voice.

"Da!" Aedan called, "the Senator is in danger!" He hoped his father understood him, and was relieved to hear his father yell, calling all Romans to his aid. As Aedan turned to prepare to fight anyone that tried to get past a large man hit him from the side.

Aedan turned, trying the pin the man against the wall. They stumbled together through the door and Aedan had to work to keep his balance. They both fell, the large man hit the ground and Aedan landed on top of him. Aedan tried the shift his sword to a position where he could stab the man. In the light of the fire, he could see the man's face. It was Cador.

Aedan scrambled to his feet and Cador got up. Aedan stared at his brother who quickly rushed off into the darkness by the wall. Aedan was startled again by a blood curdling cry. He turned again to the Senators room and was pushed aside as a stream of men rushed out. They were met by a group of legionnaires being led by his father.

Aedan was bodily pushed aside as the doorway became a portal of death. He wondered what Cador had been doing in that room. Had he been trying to rescue the Senator too? Was he part of the group that had attacked the inn? Aedan rushed along the wall of the courtyard, trying to find his younger brother. The courtyard was now littered with the dead and dying. No sign of Cador.

Chapter 9

The last body was loaded onto a wagon to be taken out of the inn. Aedan walked around the courtyard looking at the mess that had been left by the fight. He looked up at the sky, the sun was coming over the top of the wall, he had not been to sleep since the fight began. He felt that if he closed his eyes, he would only see the Senator's face.

They had found the Senator tied up, lying on his bed. His throat had been slit, and his face was still contorted in fear. Aedan had seen the body and then rushed outside to empty the contents of his stomach. The legionaries who were left helped remove the Senator before any other clean up could start. Most of the Senator's entourage went with him, leaving a few legionaries and a clerk.

Aedan went to the well in the middle of the courtyard and sat down on the wall. There was a bloody handprint on the wall, he moved to get away from it and found another one on the table close to where he sat. He looked down at his hand and realized it was bleeding again. The cloth he had used to wrap it was soaked through, he would need another soon.

Seren was calling for him, but Aedan didn't have the strength to get up from the well wall. He just sat there staring at his hands. He could hear his sister, she stopped calling for him and was now calling for his father. Her father. Their father. Good. He could help, Aedon felt he was no good to anyone.

Strong hands grabbed him by the shoulders and lifted him to his feet. His legs buckled but he could feel himself being lifted. Held in the strong arms. He looked up and saw his father's face looking down at him. Aedan thought how much his father looked like Cador. That had always bothered him. Cador got the height, muscles and looks. He got the brains. Little good that did him last night.

"Aedan," his father was saying, "come. You need to have your hand looked at." Aedan felt his father lifting him off the ground and carrying him like a baby. He wanted to snuggle into his father like he had as a child. He was a man now; he couldn't do that.

Aedan was laid down on a mat in the kitchen, close to the fire. Seren took his hand and removed the cloth. A man wearing a red tunic came over and offered him some wine with some herbs. Aedan drank and felt very sleepy. He tried to keep his eyes open to watch the man start to pull out a needle. Aedan wondered what he was going to do with it as his eyes finally closed.

When Aedan woke up his hand was wrapped in cloth again, but it was white and clean. Aedan was still on a mat in the kitchen, and he could hear his mother talking softly. He sat up but got very dizzy and had to lie down again.

"Aedon," Eira said, coming to her son's side. "You need to rest a while longer. The Medicus castrensis sewed your hand. The cut was deep. He says it will take time to heal." Aedan hadn't realized that the medical man from the legion had been here. Maybe he had been called to come after the fight.

"How long have I been asleep?" Aedon said.

"Since yesterday," Eira answered. "You don't need to worry about anything; your father and I can take care of everything." Aedan lay back down and looked around, the inn was usually a busy place, but now it stood practically empty.

Rian was using a bucket to throw water onto the dirt floor of the courtyard. Corin was fixing the door to the room where the Senator had died. Seren was hanging linens on a line by the stove to dry. Hilarus was standing by the stove, stirring something in a cauldron. Elen was bringing up more water from the well.

"Where is Cador?" Aedan asked.

"We haven't seen him," Eira said softly. "Your father thought he saw him during the fight. He wasn't among the wounded, or the dead. He's just gone." Aedon lay back again and thought about what he had seen that night.

"I need to talk to Da," Aedon said quietly, "alone if possible." Aedon didn't want to bother his mother and had to tell someone what he had seen. His father would know what to do. Eira nodded and went to fetch Corin. When she came back, she made sure they had some privacy.

"What is it son?" Corin asked as he sat on a stool by Aedan's mat. Aedan could see that his father's hands were raw with work. He had a few bruises on his face from the fight.

"During the fight," Aedan started, "in the Senator's room."

"You did well to bring attention to it," Corin said. "We were almost in time to save him."

"Yes." Aedan took a deep breath, he thought back to the look on Cador's face. He looked guilty. How could he say anything? "Cador was in the room."

"He was with you?" Corin asked, "helping you fight?"

"No," Aedan said slowly, "he was in there before. I think he was with them. Not fighting them."

"Are you sure?" Corin leaned forward and looked his son in the eye.

"Yes," Aedan said quickly, then thought about it, "no. I'm not sure why he was there. He ran away right before you joined us." Corin's head fell, he took a deep breath and then stood up.

Without saying another word, he walked back across the courtyard and started working on the door again. Aedan wondered if he had done the right thing.

The morning was far from restful as Aedan watched everyone work to get the inn clean and ready for guests again. He had always been involved in the work and now he had to watch. By afternoon, he felt well enough to sit, so his parents helped him into a chair where he could sit with a wax tablet and work out some of the financial loss caused by the damage. The gate to the courtyard opened and all heads turned to see if it was Cador.

Caela and her father entered the courtyard and Aedan had mixed feelings. He was happy to see her and yet he had hoped Cador would return. They came over to the table where Aedan sat, and Caela sat opposite him while her father greeted him and then went to see if he could help Corin.

"I heard you were hurt in the battle," Caela said. "You are so brave." Aedan blushed.

"I wasn't really," Aedan said, "I just did what I felt needed to be done." Aedan wasn't sure why he had said that he could just let her think he was a brave warrior. She smiled and put a hand on his hurt hand. He wanted to cry out in pain as she wrapped her fingers around it but didn't want her to think she had done something wrong. She was just trying to help.

"I came as soon as I heard," Caela said.

"Thank you," Aedon was in so much pain. He gently pulled his hand back and laid it in his lap. Caela looked a little offended, Aedan wondered if she had heard that he hurt his hand.

"I had to have my hand stitched," Aedan said, thinking that would make her understand.

"Yes, I heard," Caela said. "You're just so brave."

His mother and sister were by the stove. Aedan wished Caela would decide to speak with them. Of course she was here to see him. He decided to try to figure out what he could say when he saw a messenger enter the inn to bring a message to his father. After reading the message, his father rushed over to the kitchen to find Eira.

Aedan excused himself and stood to go join his parents. He was not too steady on his feet, looking at Caela who was just staring at him he decided to be brave and walk over to his parents. He was hoping they had news about Cador. When he got to where his sister was standing, she glared at him.

"You aren't supposed to be walking," Serene said sternly.

"Shush," Aedan said, then turned to his parents. "What's the message?"

"Titus and Druscilla are on their way," Corin said, "they should be here at sunset." Aedan felt his legs give and Serene caught him before he fell. She helped him walk back to the table where Caela was sitting. Serene sat with them for a moment, talking with Caela so Aedan could catch his breath. Titus and Druscilla were coming; he wondered if Maeli would be with them.

Chapter 10

As the wagon pulled up to the arch of the inn, the sun was ready to set. In the twilight, Maeli helped Druscilla step down from the wagon and then followed her into the caupona. Maeli had overheard some of the tale of what had happened, a group of Britons had broken into the inn at night and killed the Senator. It must have been a large group, as there were ten legionaries sleeping in the courtyard. Maeli looked around, it didn't look like anything had happened here. Everything was so peaceful.

During the ride up, Maeli kept wondering about Aedon. Had he been hurt in the attack, killed? She knew that Druscilla liked him, surely if he were dead she would be mourning. Maybe Druscilla hadn't been given that news yet. She shouldn't care; she barely knew him. She realized that she did care. As they entered the courtyard, Maeli looked for him. She found him sitting in the kitchen, with his betrothed.

Maeli knew that made sense; his betrothed should be here. She quickly turned back to the wagon to fetch the luggage. They had left swiftly, so Maeli had only had time to place a few things in a basket. She pulled that out and went to find Druscilla's room. They would be staying in two rooms; the Senator's room would remain empty.

Maeli organized the clothes and jewelry from the basket and came back out.

Aedan's betrothed was saying goodbye to everyone, the sun was setting and she should go home. Maeli watched her leave with a secret sense of happiness. She was jealous that the girl was allowed to just sit with Aedan. Druscilla was calling for Maeli to join her at the baths.

"Dear," Druscilla said, "I'm going to get cleaned up. Eira and Serene are joining me. Aedan has been injured in the attack." Maeli nodded, it was a surprise to her, but she kept a straight face. "Please sit with him until we return." Maeli nodded and the three ladies walked into the baths. Maeli could swear she saw Seren wink at her as she went by.

Maeli rushed across the courtyard, trying not to look like she was rushing. Aedan looked up and saw her coming and his face lit up. She took a seat at the table and smiled.

"I have been ordered to sit with you," Maeli said, "I hear you are hurt."

"I cut my hand," Aedan said, "the medicus had to stitch it."

"That sounds painful," Maeli said.

"It is," Aedan looked at his hand, still covered, and throbbing.

"You need to take your mind off it," Maeli said. "That's what my Da always said when I was hurt."

"That would be nice," Aedan said.

"My Da told me this story once when I was hurt," Maeli said. "The great hunter Brennos went to the stone where three paths meet to find the men who buried his father without song. He wanted to know if vengeance would make his clan strong or kill it." Aedan watched Maeli as she told the story. Her face came alive as she talked. He concentrated on her face; her nose was straight but had a little curve up at the end and her jawline was firm but feminine.

"He walked to the stone," Maeli continued, "one step for blood, one step for land and a third for memory. He didn't dare take a fourth step, that was for forgetting. The stone did not speak, but the wind changed and the ice on the river cracked." Maeli made a loud noise, sounding like ice cracking. She giggled a little, "my Da liked making that noise. Am I helping?" Her look was so earnest, Aedan nodded his head.

"I've forgotten," Aedan said, "like the fourth step."

"Good," Maeli laughed, it was melodic, "so nature had given Brennos a sign. At night he dreamt his father was a hill, with a wounded side. Out of that wound came children. Those yet to be born. Brennos woke and instead of gathering warriors, he gathered names." Maeli's eyes lit up. Aedan looked into those eyes; they were the color of the sea. How had he not noticed that before?

"He gathered the names of those who had gone before. Mothers as well as fathers. He spoke those names aloud to everyone he met. When the people who had killed his father to take the land came, nobody would listen to them. They did not know the names of those whose blood made the land." Maeli put her hand out for Aedan to take it. He used his good hand and put it in hers. "Without a drop of blood spilled, Brennos the Hunter claimed his land."

"What a great story," Aedan said. Maeli smiled. She looked into his dark brown eyes. Everything around them just disappeared, she was no longer a slave sold by this man. She was a girl, in love with this man.

"What's going on here?" Maeli pulled her hand back quickly as she saw a man coming over to them. She had seen him before but didn't know him. She hoped he wouldn't tell Druscilla.

"Da," Aedan said to the man as he slowly pulled his hand back. "This is Maeli. She was telling me a story to help forget the pain."

"Just a story?" Aedan's father looked suspiciously at them.

"Just a story," Aedan said with a smile. "About her ancestors." Corin shook his head and smiled. They heard Druscilla calling from the entrance to her room. Her bath was done and she was calling Maeli. Grateful, Maeli rushed back to the room to her Domina.

As she helped Druscilla get dressed, she thought back to Aedan. He had such a strong jaw, and his cheeks were high boned like her father's. She messed up the draping of Druscilla's palla, a long cloth that had to be set just so or it would fall off easily. She apologized and started again.

"You seem distracted child," Druscilla said gently.

"I'm sorry Domina," Maeli replied, "I'm worried about the death of the Senator, what it will mean."

"Don't you worry child," Druscilla put her arm around Maeli, "Titus and I will make sure you are cared for." Druscilla then stepped back into the courtyard. Maeli stayed a step behind as they walked back to the kitchen. A male slave was laying out food and a group reclined on benches to eat. There were the two women who joined Druscilla in the baths, Aedan and his father and Titus and Druscilla.

"I know you men have discussed the gruesome details surrounding the Senator's death," Druscilla said, "what can you tell the ladies?"

"Druscilla," Corin said with a laugh, "remember I know you, you want all the gruesome details." Maeli was shocked at how he spoke to her, but Druscilla laughed.

"Fine," Drusilla said, "but don't bore me, tell me what is important."

"We know that the group that attacked are a group of dissidents who don't approve of Romani rule," Titus said firmly.

"Apparently," Corin said, "and we think they came to capture the Senator, not kill him."

"That makes sense," Druscilla said.

"When Aedan brought attention to them," Corin continued, "they were trapped and decided to cut his throat." Maeli was a bit shocked at how they spoke but was impressed that Aedan had been a part of the fight. She looked at him and noticed he was a bit pale.

"Goodness," Druscilla said, then turned to Aedan, "it is important that you tried to help." Aedan nodded, broke off a piece of bread and put it on the table in front of himself.

"The problem we have, more than anything," Eira said, "we don't know where Cador has gone."

"I'm afraid we have to assume he was part of the attack," Corin said. All eyes turned to him except Aedan's. Maeli noticed that he was staring at his hand.

"What do you mean?" Eira asked incredulously.

"Aedan?" Corin looked at his eldest, "why don't you share what you saw."

"I'm not sure," Aedan said, "it was loud and a lot was happening. But Cador was in that room before I got there, and he ran when I called out for help." Maeli could see tears forming in Aedan's eyes. Seren put an arm around his shoulders, Maeli wished she could put an arm around him and hold him.

"We need to know if there is any more evidence against the boy," Titus said calmly. "He might be a victim of circumstance. Has he been keeping company with anyone in the village?" Everyone looked around the table.

"He is usually here working," Seren said, "he doesn't even go to the market." This comment brought something to Aedan's mind.

"The poacher!" Aedan exclaimed.

"What poacher?" Titus asked.

"I saw him give money to a man," Aedan said quickly, "Cador said he was a poacher. But he never brought any meat!"

"Can you describe the poacher?" Corin asked, leaning forward.

"He was about my height," Aedan started, trying to think back. "He had scars on his face. It looked like he had been melted."

"Bran," Eira said with a gasp.

"It might not be," Corin said quickly, putting a hand on Eira's shoulder.

"How many men have survived being burned like that?" Eira said.

"Who is Bran?" Titus asked. Eira looked around the table. These were people that she knew and trusted. Only Corin knew about Bran. She had never told anyone else about her brother.

"He's her brother," Corin said. "He was hurt in a fire the day we were captured. We haven't seen him in years." Eira tears in her eyes, she took her husband's hand and held it.

"Years ago, he tried to get us to join the resistance," Eira said, "but we didn't dare."

"Why not?" Maeli blurted out quickly. She immediately regretted her impulse as all eyes went to her. For a moment she had forgotten her place.

"Mind your tongue girl," Titus said harshly.

"She's right though," Druscilla said, "you were taken from your homes as children and dragged across the world to work for my family. You didn't feel that Roma was to blame for that?"

"At first," Corin admitted, "but it later became something else." He looked to Eira for help.

"We got you," Eira said, her free hand going across the table to touch Druscilla's hand that had been resting on the table. "When we moved here with you, Corin and I were given a gift better than anything. If that meant keeping allegiance with Roma, then we wanted that."

"Then when Aedan, Cador and Seren came," Corin added, "we didn't want to endanger them by turning against Roma."

"Roma has bright you great advantages," Titus said with a touch of pride.

"I don't know that everyone agrees with that," Druscilla said softly. She turned to Maeli and beckoned her to stand close. Maeli slowly stepped forward, unsure what her Domina would say. "Child? Are you happy with how we have treated you?"

"You have been kind," Maeli said, "I would like to have my freedom, but the gods have made me a slave." She heard a low noise coming from Afer, who was standing behind Titus. "I was already a slave when bought by Romani traders."

"Exactly" Titus said and immediately regretted it as Druscilla glared at him. Druscilla turned back to Maeli.

"Dear child," Druscilla said, "you are so special to me. I'm happy you've joined my household." She put an arm around Maeli and squeezed her. Maeli quietly moved back to her place. She realized that Aedan was still watching her, his expression was one of compassion. He was born a Roman citizen; he never had to worry about becoming a slave.

Maeli stood watching Aedan as the conversation continued. She was half listening, half dreaming of a life with Aedan. She imagined sitting around a fire with him at night. Being able to lay her head on his chest as they watch the flames dance for them. She wondered if he was thinking the same thing.

"It's getting late," Druscilla finally said, "we had a long journey today. We won't solve any problems tonight." Druscilla stood and continued, "I think we should get some rest and try to decide how to find Cador in the morning." Maeli followed Druscilla back to her room.

After Druscilla was ready for bed, Maeli was excused to go eat and get some sleep. She stepped into the courtyard and saw Aedan laying on a mat by the kitchen fire. The embers were glowing, casting a red light onto his face. She could tell that he was awake and staring into the embers. She slowly crossed the courtyard to join him.

"Can I join you," Maeli asked quietly. Aedan startled and turned. She could see he had tears welling up in his eyes. He wiped them with his arm and sat up a little.

"Of course," Aedan said with a sad smile. "I was just thinking about that story you told."

"What about it?" Maeli asked, she had just told the first story she remembered and didn't think much about what it meant.

"We have a proud history in Britannia," Aedan said, "our ancestors are buried in the soil here, they are part of the land. What if Cador is right?" Maeli sighed as she sat down on the mat, next to Aedan.

"He might be right," Maeli said softly, "but to kill a guest of your father? That goes against what I was taught."

"That is true for me as well," Aedan said. He sat up a little higher and looked into Maeli's eyes, the soft glow from the fire made her hair look like flames. He reached up and touched her hair, soft and cool despite the appearance of fire. "If it hadn't been for your hair I would have never met you." Maeli put a hand on his hand.

"I don't understand," Maeli said softly.

"I don't like the slave market," Aedan explained, "I was rushing by when I saw the red hair. Then I saw you, being laughed at by those monsters." Aedan took a deep breath. "You are beautiful." He leaned towards her; she didn't pull away. He looked at her hair, her eyes and her lips. He leaned further and kissed her. She wrapped her arms around his neck and kissed him back.

Part II

Discovering Freedom
(2 years later)

Chapter 11

Cador put his hands up to the fire, the cold weather was coming, and he missed the shelter of his cubiculum at the caupona. With it built above the kitchen it never got cold. The roundhouse he had built with Bran was drafty and never felt warm in the cold months. He wrapped his cloak around himself and looked over at Bran who was fast asleep.

He thought back to the day of the failed kidnapping. He had come up with the plan and paying for the men to help, Cador felt it was really going to succeed. The plan was simple; he would open the gate for the ten men that Bran hired. He had trusted this uncle who he met in the village to be able to find capable men. The plan for three of them to enter the Senator's room and tie him up quietly failed when one of the other men who was to keep watch let out a loud sneeze. The guard was alerted and the rest just fell apart.

Bran had suggested they leave their home for a land where Romans were not in power. They ran north and found a home in Caledonia. Cador had lost everything because of a sneeze. He put another log on the fire and looked out the door; the sun was starting to come up.

Cador would have to go out soon and milk the cow for Talorc. He was grateful that Talorc had taken them in, but he was a harsh taskmaster who didn't like anyone that did not do all their tasks quickly. Cador put on his leather shoes and decided to head over to the grain store to get the cows grain prepared. One his way past Bran's bed he intentionally nudged the bed to wake him.

"Morning," Cador said loudly as he pushed past the wooden door and out into the severe cold. He walked over to the small wooden building where the grain was stored as the sun started to light up the sky. He filled a bucket with grain and walked to the byre, a small shelter attached to Talorc's house.

The cow was already complaining, it's low sounds filling the air. As Cador put the grain into the trough the cow ambled over to eat. The cow always fought being milked, so Cador tied her back legs together before starting. As the first streams of white milk came from the cow, Cador saw Lirra enter the byre.

Lirra was Talorc's youngest daughter, she was tall and slender, with light brown hair that curled around her face whenever she had it down like she did now. She walked over to where the chickens were roosting and knocked them away gently to collect the eggs they had laid. As she walked back to the house she patted the cow's rump.

"Good morning, Matha," Lirra said before moving on. Matha was the name of the cow, Cador noted that she completely ignored his presence. He shook his head and smiled to himself as he continued the milking, as the youngest of five girls she had watched her sisters marry men they couldn't tolerate. She avoided most men and kept to herself.

Cador thought she was beautiful and would like to marry her but was in no position to suggest it to her. He finished milking the cow and took the bucket of milk to the main house where Talorc's wife, Una received it gracefully. She was a kind person, but Cador often wondered how a beauty like Lirra came from parents and unattractive as Talorc and Una.

"Thank you, Cador," Una said, "Talorc has some things he needs to you to deliver." Talorc was a leather worker and often asked Cador to deliver leather goods to different families in the area. Cador was expected to return with the things they exchanged in trade. It was all done on verbal agreement and memory. He thought about Aedan and his wax tablets, the constant record keeping necessary when working with Roman coins. The old way was better.

Cador walked over to the small shelter where Talorc worked on his craft. Talorc was standing at a table, his long red beard plaited down his chest and his bare arms rippling as he ran sinew through the leather he was stitching together. His face had a scar running from his hairline across his right cheek. A remnant of his days as a warrior. He limped around the table to align the pieces better. One leg had been broken in battle and healed shorter than the other.

"Una said you had work for me?" Cador asked.

"Yes," Talorc said, his voice was deep and booming. Cador often imagined it echoing across the battlefield, putting fear into the hearts of the enemy. "I have this war-coat ready for Galan." Talorc said pointing to a leather breast piece made of thick leather designed to protect from spears and arrows. Galan was the chief of the warrior clan that lived nearby and protected the village. Talorc had spent time mastering his craft after being injured and the war-coat was embossed with the symbols of the land.

"What do I take in trade?" Cador asked, caressing the hard leather.

"He has offered two young cows for it," Talorc said, "Uni added a quilted undercoat that I stitched in." He limped over and picked it up, turning it lovingly. Cador saw the wool undercoat that was a part of the war-coat adding warmth and comfort. "It is my best work."

Cador carefully took the war-coat and carried it out to the path to the village. When they had come here two years ago, Cador had been amazed at how green and beautiful the hills were. When they arrived here these hills had been dotted with the purple flowers of the thistle. He was torn apart inside, but the beauty of this place made him think everything would work out.

He thought back to the day they had met the old warrior, Talorc on this very path. Desperate, he and Bran had asked for food and shelter. Talorc had offered them a place to build a roundhouse and food if they would help him. A man with five daughters, four of them married and running their own homes had little help. Cador helped without complaining, appreciating the time spent with Lirra. Bran, however, spent most of his time in the roundhouse or the village drinking ale.

Galan lived well as the leader of the warrior clan. He had several roundhouses built around a stone broch. The broch was a stone tower that grew out of the ground like a spike. It was the fortress for his clan when trouble came. Cador had not been inside the broch, but it seemed like a cold and uncomfortable place.

Galan was sitting on a big chair in a courtyard between the houses and the broch. The chair was big and ornate, decorated with a boar head. The man himself was like a boar, he was shorter than most men, with broad shoulders. His hair was even the color of a boar, but his was long and was in several plaits on his shoulders. Several other members of the clan sat around him.

"Who are you?" Galan asked as Cador approached.

"I'm Cador," Cador replied, "I come from Talorc with your war-coat." Cador held up the leather armor and there was a murmur of appreciation among all the men there. One of the men approached and took it for Galan.

"Maili!" Galan shouted, and a girl walked out of one of the roundhouses. She was dressed too poorly to be a part of the household. She was likely a slave, taken from a nearby village. "Have someone fetch this man two young cows." The girl left and Cador went to follow when Galan called him back.

"I want to talk to you" Galan told Cador, "are you from around here?"

"I'm from Briton," Cador said, "I have come here with my uncle to escape the Romans."

"You are wanted by the Iron Eagle?" Galan said with a laugh, "of course you are! A man as big as you. You must be a direct descendant of the ancient ones." Cador's father had told him stories of the ancient ones, giants who built this land. He shook his head.

"My father was bigger," Cador said. Galan let out a loud laugh and the other men joined in.

"Why does the Iron Eagle want you?" Galan asked.

"I killed a Senator," Cador said with more bravado than he felt. He had not been the one to slit the man's throat. That man had died trying to escape the caupona. There was a loud cheer from the men. Galan slapped the arms of his chair and stood. Cador felt intimidated as the man walked closer even though the man barely came past his stomach. Cador was not a warrior; he had been in one fight in his life and failed miserably.

"You will join us," Galan said.

"I'm not a warrior," Cador admitted, "I murdered the man in his bed." That sounded better than admitting he tried to kidnap the man and failed.

"Your size? And the willingness to kill a man?" Galan said with a laugh. "I can teach you." Cador wasn't sure he had a choice, so he nodded his head.

"I must return the cows to Talorc," Cador said quietly.

"Does he own you?" Galan asked with sudden realization, it was possible that Cador was a slave.

"I am a free man," Cador said.

"Good," Galan said, "give my greetings to Talorc and we will meet here in the morning."

Cador walked away, unsure of what it would mean. He felt as if his fortune was about to change.

Chapter 12

Maeli walked her required one step behind Druscilla as they walked down the streets of the great city of Roma. It was crowded, dirty and it smelt bad. Maeli did not think it was so great. It had been over a year since Titus had been called back to Roma. Maeli didn't understand politics at all, but what she understood was the emperor was dead and any governors he supported were told to return to Rome. Titus had dragged them all back as well, since he had to go with the governor.

Shortly after returning, there were long meetings where Maeli had to stand behind Druscilla and wait to be told what to do. With everything happening in Latin, Maeli didn't understand half of what was going on. She often just stood and thought about Aedan and wondered what he was doing. That night in the kitchen they had shared a kiss and then talked until she couldn't keep her eyes open.

"Maeli," Druscilla said now as she walked up the street to another large building. How did she know one from another? "Keep up child." By her own reckoning, Maeli was sixteen Roman years old. She was not a child; she was a woman. Maeli caught up and they walked past another row of columns and into a big room. In front of them was a statue of a god. Which one was this? Maeli wondered.

The god was an older woman, wearing a long dress. She was brightly colored, her dress a deep purple, hair a dark brown and her crown bright gold. Maeli wondered about why the god wore a dress that hid nothing. Her legs and breasts were plain to see. She realized she had been to this temple before. This was Juno, goddess of marriage or women, Maeli never really tried to learn them.

Outside of her own gods, the only one Maeli was interested in was the Mashiach, Josephus' god that walked among men. She had sat with Josephus as he read the Greek letter a few times. He would explain some of it to her, but she still didn't fully understand. She did like the part about being a slave, the Mashiach apparently offered a different kind of slavery that led to freedom. She didn't fully understand, but the idea was interesting to her.

Druscilla told Maeli to stay behind as she made a sacrifice to the goddess. Maeli watched as Druscilla went to an altar and lit something on fire, the smoke wafted up through the air, filling the air with a powerful scent. She then took a jar from the folds of her robe and poured the contents into a bowl. Maeli knew it contained wine; she had filled it with the best wine in the domus. Druscilla stood there for a time, seemingly speaking a prayer before returning to Maeli.

"There," Druscilla said firmly, "we are done." Her duty fulfilled, Druscilla took Maeli's hand and led her away. This action of walking alongside Maeli was something Druscilla had started when she obviously needed someone to talk with. Maeli felt honored that she was so well trusted to hear the deeper thoughts of her Domina.

"My child," Druscilla continued, "today my husband faces a serious challenge. The new Emperor is a friend of the Senator killed in the caupona. He is wanting to know what happened that day." Maeli's heartbeat faster. She knew it was Aedan's brother and uncle that plotted against the Senator.

"What will Domine Titus tell him?" Maeli asked, forgetting to use his full name. If Druscilla noticed she didn't say anything.

"He hasn't told me," Druscilla said, "and I have no right to ask. Men run this empire, and it is best to remember that." She held Druscilla's hand tightly as they walked through the streets to the domus.

Josephus was ready for them in the atrium when they arrived, he looked nervous. He led them away from anywhere the slaves could hear them. This domus was much larger than the domus in

Londinium, so the corner of the room was far enough to avoid eavesdropping.

"Domina, I am afraid," Josephus said quietly. "Your husband has returned and ordered us all to stay away from his cubiculum."

"How did he act?" Druscilla sounded concerned, but Maeli didn't quite understand anything that was happening.

"Not well," Josephus said, "he looked the same as the night of the fires." Druscilla looked troubled. Maeli had heard tales of the fire that burned the great city, it was a part of why the old Emperor was not liked. That was the night that Druscilla's parents died as well. Killed in the fire.

"I see," Druscilla said, taking a deep breath. "Maeli, stay here. I will check on him." Druscilla walked across the atrium, the beauty of the plants hanging from the ceiling and the tiles on the floor ignored as she went to the entrance to the corridor that led to their cubiculum.

Maeli stood quietly, she could hear Josephus muttering something quietly in his own tongue. There was a sudden tension, and she didn't dare break it to ask what he was saying. He looked frightened. Suddenly the domus was filled with a loud scream. Josephus grabbed Maeli's hand.

"Come," Josephus said, "she will need us." He led Maeli down the long corridor. They went past several doors before they came to the entrance to the cubiculum that Druscilla shared with her husband. Druscilla was in the entrance looking in, her face a mixture of grief and fear.

"He's dead," Druscilla cried out as soon as she saw Josephus. Maeli was not sure what was going on, she put her arm around Druscilla and led her away from the door. Josephus went into the cubiculum while Maeli led Druscilla back to the atrium where there was a reclinium, a padded bench. Druscilla collapsed onto it and wept. Maeli held her waiting for Josephus to help.

"My Domina," Josephus said as he came out of the corridor, "I am so sorry." Josephus took Maeli aside and told her to take Druscilla to the other cubiculum they kept for guests. "Let her rest," Josephus added, "stay with her."

"What happened?" Maeli asked,

"He has taken his own life," Josephus said quietly. "He died with dignity instead of being executed."

"Why would he be executed?" Maeli asked, confused.

"I will explain it to you when I can," Josephus said, "until then, care for your Domina." Josephus rushed off across the courtyard to a dark corner that held the entrance to the corridor reserved for the slaves.

"Come Domina," Maeli said, putting a hand on Druscilla's shoulder, "we can go and rest in another cubiculum." Druscilla sniffed and held her head up. Her eyes were filled with resolution.

"No," Druscilla said, "I'm fine. Have Josephus come see me in my cubiculum." Druscilla stood and walked with determination to the cubiculum. Maeli quickly went to tell Josephus he was needed. As they got to the cubiculum, they found Druscilla standing over Titus' body holding a piece of parchment. She was reading what was written on it.

"It seems my sacrifice to Juno was too late," Druscilla said stoically. She placed the parchment down and turned to Josephus. "Help me clean the body, and then we will move him to the Atrium. You are excused dear," she said to Maeli.

Maeli reluctantly went to the small cubiculum where she slept. It was close to Druscilla's room so that she could be called in the night if needed. Maeli lay down on her bed and curled up into a ball. She didn't want to be here, she hated Rome. She hated this domus. She wanted to be home.

Chapter 13

The courtyard of the Caupona Caureni sat empty. Aedan sat in the kitchen with his mother counting the few coins they had left. Two legionaries stood outside the gate, telling anyone that came that the Caupona was closed and under the emperor's control.

Immediately after the Senator's death there had been a quick inquiry, and things seemed to go back to normal. They had fewer visitors, but people quickly forgot about the scandal. Then, almost a year later Titus was told to return to Roma. He came to them the night before he left and explained what he knew.

"Senator Marcus Fabius Severus, was here to raise support against Nero," Titus explained, "now Nero is gone. The faction that the Senator supported tried to gain power but failed. There has been great turmoil in Roma. We've changed emperors four times now, and the Senator's favored man now sits as emperor. He is a man that does not forget. He has ordered a full inquiry into the death of Marcus Fabius."

Shortly after Titus left a Romani official arrived with a decree announcing the closing of the caupona. The family was placed on house arrest, the slaves removed from the household and guards were stationed at the gate. They were happy they were together but were not allowed to leave the caupona.

Aedon and Eira had collected the money they had remaining and made plans for how to survive. The stable at the back had been converted to house a cow, some chickens and a few goats. Corin and Aedon had dug up most of the courtyard and planted a garden for the herbs and vegetables they needed.

Caela was permitted to visit as Aedan's betrothed and would use the coins to buy food they couldn't grow themselves. Their daily routine had gone from caring for guests to surviving. Then the day came when Caela stopped coming. After a week news came that Caela's parents had decided she had no future with Aedan and agreed to a different husband for her. They didn't have the courage to tell them; she just stopped coming.

The day someone finally told Aedan he sat in kitchen, hoping that all this was a nightmare when Seren came and sat with him. After a few minutes of silence, Seren sensed her brother needed something to lift him out of his misery.

"She wasn't good for you," Seren said. "She liked one person, and that was herself."

"I know," Aedan said sadly, "but I'm without any prospects for marriage now." Seren put a hand on her brother's hand and took in his miserable expression.

"There's always the girl with the red hair," Seren said.

"Maeli?" Aedan asked, "she's in Roma and I'm stuck here."

"Da and Ma were separated for years," Seren said. "I know you two were brought together by the gods, she will be back for you." Seren stood suddenly and kissed her brother on the cheek before rushing off to the courtyard. Aedan watched her go, her yellow hair glistening in the sunlight, wishing he had the same confidence.

That had been weeks ago and now they were almost out of money and would have to make different plans moving forward.

"We still have the beds and blankets in the guest cubicula," Aedan said. "We can sell those."

"I'm not sure I want to touch those," Eira said, "technically they belong to Druscilla as well."

"Where is she?" Aedan said sternly, "probably living comfortably in Roma while we starve to death!" Eira gave him a stern look.

"I'm sure she is doing what she can from her place!" Eira said sternly. "These things take time!"

"Have you heard from her?" Aedan asked, before Eira could answer he added, "of course not. She's not coming back." Aedan stood up and walked over to the courtyard where rain was pouring through the open roof. The rain matched his mood perfectly. Maeli had been taken to Roma with Druscilla, and he was stuck here in this run-down inn. Every night as he lay in bed, he would think back to that kiss, that moment that he had wanted to last forever.

Eira walked over to Aedan and put an arm around his shoulder. He looked at his mother and smiled at her sadly. He had not told his parents about his feelings for Maeli, they had arranged for his marriage, and it felt disrespectful to admit he wanted to marry another woman. It didn't matter anyway, he would likely never see Maeli again.

"Son," Eira said, "we are all upset, but I have confidence that Titus and Druscilla are working to make things better."

"I'm sorry," Aedan said, "it's just taking so long." Eira gave her son a quick hug and went back to the table to return the coins to the purse. Aedan walked through the rain to the stables, he would have to feed the animals soon and the rain was not letting up. As he scooped grain into the trough for the cow he thought about Cador.

The stable had always been Cador's responsibility. Aedon wondered what had gotten into his brother's head to drive him to kill the Senator. Aedan had always been proud of his family heritage, a sheep herding family that had found their place in the new Roman world, running a successful caupona. He was happy with where they were and often enjoyed spending time with the Romans who came to the inn.

The chickens were moving around, scratching the wet ground and Aedan stood there in the rain watching them. They had built a roosting box for the hens over in a corner of the stable. In that corner was a small, arced opening that led to the firebox for the bathhouse. Even though they didn't have any guests, they took turns to keep those fires lit to keep the chickens warm. Aedan checked to make sure it was going, and noticed the flames were blazing. Obviously, someone had built it up. The water in the bath was probably nice and warm.

Standing here, soaking wet, the warm bath sounded good. Aedon walked around to the entrance of the bath and walked in. The baths were a long sequence of rooms designed to be reminiscent of the large bathhouses of Roma. The first room had a small mosaic on the floor which had a pattern that matched the sign outside the gate, the three circles that seemed to be swirling around each other. Aedan undressed and put his clothes on the wooden pegs placed on the wall. He noticed his father's tunic was on another peg.

The next room of the bath was a warm room, heated by the air from the big hot room. Aedan had been taught by his mother as a boy to use a strigil, a small, curved metal tool, to scrape

the dirt and oils from his skin. As he did this, he
noticed that his body had become much more
muscular. Up to this point his life had been
calculations and making decisions about menus and
supplies. Now he was digging in the courtyard,
caring for animals and maintaining the property. He
had become very strong.

Aedan walked through the arch to the main
room of the bath. This one had copper pipes on
the walls filled with hot water and a small pool in
the middle that also had hot water. Steam filled the
room from vents on the floor. As a boy, Aedan
loved to come here on a cold winter day and run
around in the warm air. The three siblings would be
allowed to come in here to play games on rare
occasions when there were no guests. The Romani
felt it disrespectful to let children run free, but to
them it was just a good place to stay warm.

Corin was sitting on a bench close to one of
the steam vents. He had his head against the wall
and his eyes were closed. Aedan didn't want to
disturb him and gently lowered himself into the
pool of hot water. It felt so good, he hadn't realized
how cold he had been in the rain.

"Good morning," Aedan jumped when his
father spoke. He turned as his father stood and
came over to the pool. "Your mother is worried
about you," Corin said as he stepped into the pool.

"I'll be fine," Aedan said, not sure if this was true or not. "It has been a long year, not knowing what will happen."

"It has been," Corin admitted, "you and your sister have had your lives drawn to a halt before they could begin. Your mother and I know what that is like." Aedan thought about that, he had never thought about what that would be like to have your entire life uprooted because of the actions of someone else.

"How did you survive?" Aedan asked.

"By taking life a challenge at a time," Corin answered. "At first, I was obsessed with escape and trying to find a way out of the situation. When I finally decided to accept things and do what was asked of me, a situation to make my life better just came."

"I remember," Aedan loved all of his parent's stories, "you rescued Druscilla from kidnappers and had to bring her here to keep her safe."

"That's right," Corin said with a chuckle. "We need some kidnappers now," he made a menacing face, "I could defeat them and get us out of here." Aedan laughed and shook his head. He remembered playing with his father and Cador as boys. He would make these mean faces as they wrestled.

"Where do you think Cador is now?" Aedan asked and immediately regretted it when his father's face fell. Corin took a deep breath and went into a fit of coughing. When he stopped, he pulled himself out of the pool.

"Somewhere safe," Corin said, "it's hot in here, I'm going to cool off." Aedan followed his father to the final room, with the bigger pool filled with cold water. They got in and Corin immediately had another fit of coughing.

"You ok, Da?" Aedan asked.

"Just feeling the wet weather," Corin said with a smile.

Chapter 14

The group of warriors travelled through the woods, coming up on a river. On the other side of the river were about ten cows. Cador stood next to Galan, each man wearing a leather war-coat, Galan's the much more ornate one Talorc had made. They had handed their shields to other men and carried only their spears. In his free hand Cador carried a rope.

Galan nodded to Cador and the tall man waded across the river. The water was deep in the middle, coming up to his waist. When he arrived on the other shore he looked back at Galan before walking forward to where a young cow was grazing. The cow was very tame, so tying the rope around its neck was simple. As Cador led the cow back to the river it followed obediently.

The cow hesitated briefly as they came to the river but then followed Cador into the cold water. As they got a little further, Cador heard a loud cry from behind him. He didn't look back but kept moving into the water. An arrow splashed into the water next to him and Cador saw Galan stand with a bow in his hand , Galan shot an arrow that flew past Cador towards his enemy.

Cador reached the deep water and the cow struggled to keep up. He could hear someone splashing into the water behind him and saw Galan rushing forward with his spear. As soon has he got into shallow water, Cador urged the cow to the shore close to Galan and turned to face the man who was behind him.

Cador leveled his spear at the man, who stopped in his tracks just beyond the spear. This man had been caught unawares and had no shield. With just his spear, he had no way to defend himself if Cador decided to thrust his spear into him. They stood there for a moment as each man decided what to do.

"Kill him!" Galan yelled from where he stood behind Cador. Without another thought Cador thrust his spear forwards and watched it pierce the man's chest. Blood poured out from the wound and the man's hands grabbed the spear as if holding it would stop him from dying. Cador pulled back on the spear to retrieve it, the man, pulled forward by the pressure fell face first into the water.

Cador stepped backwards, looking at the man lying in the river, his blood turning the water red. He grabbed the rope again and pulled the cow onto the shore. Galan let out a cry as they rushed back into the woods. They had managed to take the cow with little resistance.

"Should we try for one more?" Cador asked, blood rushing through his veins.

"More men will be coming," Galan said. Cador followed the warrior chief through the woods where their men were waiting for them. When they saw the cow, they let up a cheer. Cador had taken his first cow and had started building his own wealth.

When they returned to the broch, Cador handed his cow to one of the slaves while the men returned to gather around Galan's big chair for a celebration. Cador felt like this was where he belonged, with those that followed the old ways.

"We can expect a raid from the river clan," Galan said loudly, he took a drink of ale and some dribbled down his beard. He ignored it and slammed his cup on the arm of his chair. "Now young Cador!" Galan continued, "we need to make you a true member of the clan!" Galan bellowed for Talorc to come forward.

Talorc limped into the circle of men, standing tall. Cador was pleased to see Lirra with him. He was not pleased to see Bran had also come. The three walked to Galan and bowed their heads in greeting.

"Galan," Talorc said, "I see your war-coat fits you well."

"It does!" Galan said. "I wore it today as we claimed our victory!" This was met with a great cheer from the men. "We have young Cador, who you brought to us, joining the clan today! You may not fight anymore, but you are keeping the clan strong!"

"Thank you," Talorc said, standing tall.

"Do you wish to move forward with our agreement?" Galan asked.

"Yes," Talorc said, looking over at Cador. Galan let out a bellowing laugh.

"Good!" Galan said, "Warrior Cador, come forward!" Cador stepped forward and stood next to Bran. "I understand you and your uncle have built a house in Talorc's lardos." The lardos was the area protected by a fence, his house was just outside the lardos, but Cador did not want to disagree.

"Yes," Cador said.

"Then you are man enough," Galan said with a laugh, "you have a house and a cow. Would you agree he is man enough Talorc?" The leatherworker nodded his head sagely. "Then it is done!"

"What is done?" Cador asked.

"Talorc has agreed with me that you should marry his daughter," Galan said. "It is our way that all warriors from outside be married to keep you loyal to the clan. Are you in agreement?" Cador gently nodded his head and glanced over at Lirra; she did not seem to be as willing to this plan. She stood glaring at the ground, her face filled with contempt. Cador was confident that in the time of his betrothal he could win her over.

"That would be a good thing;" Cador said.

"Very good!" Galan said, "you will be joined tonight!" Cador wasn't sure what to say. Bran found his voice.

"Tonight?" Bran said, "they are still young!"

"Tonight!" Galan said, "he has proven himself and had a house of his own." Galan stood up and walked up to Cador, his small stature more obvious as he stood next to the young man. "It is our way!"

"Where will I stay?" Bran said, "I cannot stay with the young couple. That is not my way." Bran emphasized the word "my," when he spoke. Galan glared at him.

"You will stay at the broch," Galan said with a tone that told Bran not to argue. "Your nephew said you were a great warrior." Bran turned to Cador.

"He did?" Bran asked.

"Of course I did," Cador replied. Cador looked at Lirra and could see a tear going down her cheek. "Galan, I do not think she wants to marry me," Cador said softly to Galan.

"She has rejected every man her father has presented," Galan said softly, "he has given her no choice." Galan slapped Cador on the back. "A warrior faces many challenges!" Galan laughed as he walked away.

By the time the sun was going down the fields around the broch were filled with people from the clan. Cador and Lirra were brought to the base of the tall grey tower, and an old Druid tied their hands together with a rope. The fiber from the rope scratched Cador's wrists as the Druid called on the gods to bless the union.

After the rope was removed a great feast was presented. Cador was impressed at how much food could be prepared in such little time. During the feast, his new wife did not speak with or even look at Cador. He tried to talk to her, but she ignored him. It became dark and the feast went late into the night. Finally, Galan stood up and raised his arms, the crowd silenced for their leader.

"We must let the newly married couple have some time tonight!" Galan said. This was met with a great cheer. Cador wasn't sure he wanted to be alone with Lirra, and he knew she didn't want to be with him. The walk back to his roundhouse was a slow and torturous walk. Lirra walked a step behind him so he could not easily speak with her.

As they passed through the doorway, Cador went to the hearth to build up the fire. Lirra looked around at the sparse belongings Cador and Bran had accumulated. She finally sat on the bed and sighed. Cador watched her unsure what to do or say. She finally stood up and turned to him.

As she started to remove her tunic, Cador realized she was reluctantly giving herself to him.

He stood quickly and put a hand on her arm, stopping her.

"You do not want to do this," Cador said. The fire was blazing now and the orange light lit up her face. Her hair and eyes were both a light brown color. Her skin was soft and almost translucent in this light. She looked at him with both hatred and pleading.

"It is my duty as your wife," Lirra said, her voice breaking as if she was about to cry.

"Your duty is to do what I want," Cador said. "You are the most beautiful woman I've seen, but I will not force you. I did not plan for us to be married like this." Cador sat on the bed and motioned for Lirra to do the same. "Once you know me, I hope you will be happy being my wife."

Lirra stared at Cador, unsure of what to say. Cador tuned and stared into the fire. He thought about the stories his mother had told him as a boy of how she had always been in love with his father. He wished he had known someone that loved him like that. He was never someone the girls would look at and whisper about. He was tall and awkward. He knew he wasn't attractive, but he had hoped that maybe Lirra would see past his flat nose and small jaw.

"Thank you," Lirra finally said. Cador stood and walked over to the other bed. It was late and he was tired. He lay down and turned his back to his

wife. As he drifted off to sleep, he could hear her
breathing deeply.

Chapter 15

They had burned the body and placed the ashes in a small building, just for the dead. Maeli wondered how Titus could return to the land from inside the building. Druscilla had kept him in the atrium of the house for two days, and then they took him out of the city to burn him. There were some people that visited, they kept whispering about the shame he brought to his family.

During those days, Druscilla kept the house dark and quiet. The day after the burning of her husband, Druscilla asked Maeli to help her find her finest clothes. After Druscilla was draped in a green pala, a long strip of fine fabric, and a white dress. She beckoned Mali to follow her out the door.

"We are heading to the Curia," Drusilla said once they got to the street. "I have been summoned, for the reading of my husband's will." The walk was a long one, and Maeli wondered what she meant by Titus' will. She realized she really didn't know much about how things worked in this confusing place. A woman was summoned so soon after her husband's death. And for what. Reading something. It made no sense to her.

In her home, a woman was given time to mourn. Her family would care for her and not make her do anything she didn't want to. Maeli noticed that the buildings around her were getting larger. They were in the heart of Roma and there were pillars so tall she could barely see the top. So many people were here as well.

Maeli followed Druscilla into a building that in her mind looked like a cave. The roof was arched up and looked like the roof of one of the caves she had explored when she was a child. The people here were solemn, Maeli wondered if some of them had ever smiled. They came to a large chamber in the building with a chair high on a platform. Sitting in the chair was an old man wearing a purple toga. He was balding and his stomach pushed his tunic as far as it could go. Maeli might have laughed if she wasn't so much in awe of the place. Maeli stayed one step behind Druscilla but wished she could hide away. The air felt tense in the room.

"Druscilla Flavius Severus," the man in the chair said. The people in the room fell silent.

"That is me," Druscilla said. She took a deep breath, and stood tall as the man removed a wax seal from a scroll and opened it. Everyone waited quietly while he read.

"On the passing of your husband," the man read aloud, "due to his guilt regarding the murder of Senator Marcus Falvius the emperor has seized all of his property." Druscilla gasped. Titus had left her a letter saying he took responsibility for the death of the Senator. She didn't really think about the legal consequences.

"That will include the domus in Roma and Londinium, the country villa and the slaves will be sold and the money given to the great city." Druscilla looked faint, her skin was so pale. Maeli positioned herself to catch her if she fainted. Druscilla remained standing tall.

"I see," Druscilla said softly, "I am left with nothing." The man in the chair still had more to read so he held up his hand for silence.

"Your property was divided," the man said reading, "when you married, all you owned was left in your name. Titus said that you were not involved in the murder, so the Emperor has laid no claim on your property. You are dismissed." Maeli followed Druscilla out of the room. She thought back to the whole thing, it seemed unreal. From what she understood the emperor was going to take her house and sell the slaves. Maeli wondered what would happen to her.

It was a long walk back to the domus, Druscilla was unsure who to turn to. Her parents were dead; her husband was gone. She was left with what she had brought into the marriage. She couldn't remember what that was, the stress of the moment made thinking impossible.

Maeli was lost in her own thoughts. She would be sold again. She prayed that they did not humiliate her by making her remove her tunic, again. The last time she had been young and thin, she didn't have much of a figure to cover. Now she had become a woman and knew she would attract the attention of men. That couldn't be good.

When they arrived back home, there were already people removing items from the domus. Josephus was standing in the atrium looking lost as furniture was being taken. When he saw the ladies arrive, he rushed over.

"I'm sorry Domina" Josephus said quickly, "they came and removed all the slaves except me and started to remove the furniture."

"Why are you still here?" Maeli blurted out. Druscilla didn't even seem to notice the breach of etiquette as she stood and watched her belongings leave the domus.

"I wasn't on the list," Josephus explained, "they took the slaves owned by Domine Titus, you and I belong to Domina Druscilla." Maeli did not really understand any of this. She just stared blankly at Josephus. "I was inherited after the fire, everything else was gone, I was all she inherited. She bought you from Aedan using her own money. They are only taking what is his."

"The fire!" Druscilla said suddenly coming to life. "I also inherited the country villa. Titus took care of it, but it remains mine." Druscilla took off towards her cubiculum so fast Maeli and Josephus had to run to catch up. The room was still untouched, and Druscilla pointed to a chest she kept in the corner. "Fill that with clothes Maeli," she said.

"Yes Domina," Maeli said, happy with something to do. She took all the clothes from shelves and off pegs in the room and put them as neatly as she could into the chest. Druscilla pulled out her coin purse and handed Josephus a few coins.

"Hire a wagon and send it here and then take a chariot to my father's country place." Druscilla said, "we will be there shortly after." She looked around at the cubiculum, before adding, "there is nothing more for me here." Josephus rushed from the cubiculum, obviously happy to have something to do.

Before long all the clothes were packed. Druscilla collected her combs and other personal items she had. Once all was in the chest, the men came to the door to collect the furniture. They agreed to carry Druscilla's chest out and leave it on the road. It wasn't long before Druscilla and Maeli were standing on the road, with only a chest of clothing.

When the wagon arrived, the driver helped Maeli load the chest and they left the domus behind. Maeli was impressed that Druscilla did not look back as they drove away from her home. She looked so regal sitting in the wagon there would be no way to guess she had just lost everything. The ride to the country villa took a little under an hour, Maeli had never been to this villa before. It was nestled into a valley; the land was well kept.

When they pulled up to the actual villa, they could see it was not as well maintained as the land. The plaster on the walls was cracking and there were clay shingles laying on the ground that had come from the roof. Druscilla let out a long sigh.

"I used to love coming here as a child," Druscilla said. "I haven't been here in a long time. Titus put people on the land, but obviously just let the villa sit." Druscilla got off the wagon and walked up to the entrance to the villa. The door was hanging off one hinge; she found a bench by the door and sat on it. Maeli helped the driver remove the crate and the wagon turned around and left.

Josephus appeared in the entryway, behind the half-broken door. He pushed his way past the door, being careful not to move it too much.

"My Domina," Josephus said, "the villa has been raided by thieves. There is little left inside." Druscilla let out a little laugh.

Druscilla stood up and with Jospehus' help entered the villa. Maeli followed. The door led to a large atrium, with an open roof. This had given plants the sunlight and water they needed to take over the space. What had obviously been a beautiful mosaic on the floor was torn up by the roots of young trees. Grass was also starting to grow in the sunlit areas.

"My mother loved this atrium," Druscilla said. "She would spend hours tending to the plants that grew here. I suppose it's only right they have kept the place alive." Druscilla walked across the atrium slowly to the entrance to the back corridor. They walked down, it was dark and damp, but Maeli could imagine that at one time it was filled with light from the lamps and warm.

As they came to the first entry, they looked inside. The ceiling had collapsed and they could see roof tiles and a few places the sun poked through. There was no furniture indicating what the room might be for. Druscilla just shook her head and moved along the corridor.

The next room had an ornate door; it was deeply carved with images of trees and animals. Druscilla gently pushed the door open. The ceiling was intact, but there was definite damage done by water coming through the tiles. There was a bed lying broken in the middle of the room.

"My parents' cubiculum," Druscilla said with a light laugh. "I never came in here, except once when my mother brought me in to show me the brooch my father bought her." They went on down the corridor. They passed a few more entrances before coming to the last cubiculum in the corridor.

"This was my room," they went through the door and were amazed to find the room looked undamaged. There was a mural of animals playing on the wall, which was faded but still visible. There was a bed up against the far wall, that looked sound. They walked in and Druscilla looked around. The room looked like the thieves had not touched it. There was still a wool blanket on the bed, clothes on the shelf and a mat on the floor.

"It hasn't changed," Druscilla said, a smile coming to her face. "This was my bed, and there" she pointed to the mat on the floor "was where Eira slept." Druscilla stood looking at the mat. When she and Eira came here they would spend the days running out in the fields looking for the shepherd that Eira was in love with. At night Eira would tell her stories of her childhood, playing with Corin the shepherd boy.

Druscilla looked at that mat and thought about the Eira. She and Corin had rescued Druscilla and taken her to Brittania to escape men that wanted her dead. They had been the ones to raise her while living in her father's Caupona in Britannia.

"The Caupona Caureni!" Druscilla
exclaimed. Maeli didn't understand, but Josephus
clapped his hands a single time.

"Yes!" Josephus said. "It is your property."

"The emperor won't have taken it!"
Druscilla concluded. Maeli still wasn't sure what
was going on but she could tell that they had found
something to be happy about.

"What does that mean?" Maeli asked.

"It means we can go back to Brittania!"
Druscilla said, "Corin and Eira are the only family I
have left, and I can find a place with them." Maeli
finally understood what they were saying. She was
going back to Aedan.

Chapter 16

"The Romans are gone!" Seren was running up the stairs shouting, "the Romans are gone!" Aedan cracked his head on a low beam sitting up in his bed. Corin came out of his room and rushed past Corin who was holding his head.

"What do you mean?" Corin asked Serene as she burst into the room.

"There are no legionaries at the door!" Serene said, "they left this nailed to the door." She lifted an official looking document and Corin took it from her. Eira stumbled into the room, looking tired and disheveled. Corin started to read but had a fit of coughing again.

"Are you alright?" Eira asked. Corin handed her the document and continued to cough.

"I'm fine," he said between coughing, "you read it." Eira looked concerned but took the document.

"It says that we have been found not guilty of the murder of the Senator," Eira read. "They have found the guilty," Eira stumbled over the word, "guilty person." She paused for a moment the whispered, "Cador." Corin took the document and read it himself.

"It might not be Cador," Corin said, "it says one person was arrested, Cador was just one of them. There were at least twenty men. They probably caught the leader." He stopped when he realized that it was likely Bran. Bran had encouraged his son to join this attack, Corin secretly hoped it was Bran. Corin put the document on the table. This meant they could open for business. He wanted to say something but started coughing again.

"Corin," Eira said, "that cough is getting worse, I wish you would visit the medicus in town." Corin waved the suggestion off. The last thing he wanted was a Roman medicus poking at him and taking his blood away. He had visited a Druid and had been given some herbs. They would work given time.

"I'll be fine," Corin said. "We need to get this place running again." Aedan got out of bed, excited about having paying guests again. They needed to make sure there was enough food and other necessities. They should get some food prepared for any guests that may be traveling through today. That's when he realized something.

"We have no slaves," Aedan said, "can we run this place without them?" Corin and Eira exchanged a look. They had kept the slaves because that was considered a part of running the inn. When they had been taken away by the Romans, there was a sense of loss but also personal freedom.

"Seren and I can run the kitchen," Eira said.

"I can work in the stable," Corin said. His cough threatened to come back, but he managed to suppress it. "I will need a little help."

"I think I can manage to help," Aedan said. They all rushed to get dressed and went downstairs to get things ready. Eira and Seren got a big fire going in the kitchen hearth. They went through the supplies and found they had enough to make some flat bread. Corin suggested they butcher some of the chickens to have them ready.

The courtyard would take some time to get ready, since they had dug up half of it for the garden. Corin and Aedan started cleaning it up so there were good paths through the garden. They did not want to remove all the plants as they still didn't have enough money to buy what they needed.

By midday Corin was feeling a bit weak. He wondered if he could manage the stable alone. He might need help, but he wasn't going to force someone to work for him. There had to be someone who could help him. Corin sat down on a bench and considered who he knew, that would be willing to take up the challenge of getting an inn running again.

Corin watched his family hard at work. He had to get back to work. He stood up to start back and felt a sudden weakness. Feeling dizzy, he tried to sit and missed the bench. When he hit the ground, he felt all the air go out of him. He tried to stand up but felt everything go dark. He fell back and could feel the cool soil beneath him. He could hear someone calling his name.

Eira had seen Corin collapse and rushed to his side. She called Aedan over and the two of them managed to get him to one of the guest rooms. Once they had him in bed, Eira sent Aedon to fetch the medicus from the nearby Roman fort. It would take him at least an hour to get there and back. Eira prayed to the gods he would make it in time.

Seren came to the entry and looked in. She had brought a cup of wine, thinking that might help. Eira was proud of her children, they never panicked. Seren went in and put her hand on her father's cheek.

"He's hot," Seren said. Eira walked over and felt Corin's cheek. He was hot. She was really worried now; a fever was serious.

"Come," Eira said, "we must get some cold cloth, cool him down." Eira and Seren took some cloth and used water from the well to get it damp and cool. They took it to Corin and put it across his brow and across his chest to cool him down. "You get back to work on the bread," Eira finally said, "I'll sit with your father." As Seren left, Eira pulled a chair over close to the bed and sat with her husband.

She thought back to the day they had been betrothed. She had been begging her father to let her marry Corin, he was so big and strong. She had loved the way he smiled when he told stories about his sheep. Her father had finally agreed after Bran had fallen and hurt himself, Corin had agreed to watch both flocks of sheep without asking anything in return.

Their actual marriage ceremony was a little less than she had expected. With their families gone, and them enslaved in Roma, they were married in the slave quarters of their master's domus. Their first time together was in that same cramped place, cut short by the need to return to work.

Seren came to the door again, behind her was a man she had never seen before. He didn't look like a medicus. Eira stood and walked over to see them. The man looked familiar, but she couldn't quite place him.

"Ma," Seren said, "Owain is here." Eira realized that's why he looked familiar. Owain was a boy from the area, the son of a farming family. He and Seren played together when they were young. He had become a man in the year they were imprisoned.

"Hello Owain," Eira said, "I'm sorry we are not able to have guests. My husband isn't well"

"Seren told me," Owain said, his voice much deeper than Eira was expecting. "Is there anything I can do?"

"Nobody has had time to milk the cow," Seren said. Eira was about to argue that it could wait and send the boy away, but realized Seren was right.

"I can do that," Owain said with a smile.

"I would be grateful for your help," Eira said. Owain rushed off to the stable to milk the cow.

"Thanks Ma," Seren said before rushing off to get back to the bread cooking by the fire. Eira returned to her chair and checked to make sure the cloth was still cool. Corin felt a little cooler now, and his breathing was calm. She felt confident that the medicus could bring him back to health.

The time seemed to stand still. Eira could hear Owain and Seren talking as they did various tasks around the courtyard. She was aware things were happening around her, but all she could think of was Corin. Aedan was taking his time getting the medicus.

Fortunately, the medicus was given use of a chariot and they were back to the cauperna swiflty. As they arrived Eira explained what had happened while the medicus examined Corin.

"His humors are out of balance," the medicus said sternly, "I will need to balance them."

He took a sharp knife and cut into Corin's skin on the forearm. As the blood started to run out of the cut, he collected it into a clay bowl he had brought. After the correct amount of blood had been removed, he bandaged the arm with a white cloth. "I will be back tomorrow to check on him," the medicus said before heading out to the waiting chariot.

Eira looked at Corin, wondering if releasing his humors would work. He looked peaceful laying there. She prayed to the gods that he would wake up soon. Aedan was standing by the bed as all this happened. His face was ashen, he looked worried.

"Aedan," Eira said, "Owain is out there with your sister. Can you make sure everything is going alright? We still need to get this place ready so we can open." Eira hoped that would distract him from worrying about Corin. Aedan nodded his head and rushed out without another word.

Chapter 17

The roundhouse was empty when Cador woke up. A small part of him wondered if he had dreamed the whole thing. He was now married to Lirra, and still his home was empty. He stood up and went to the hearth where the embers were still glowing. He built up the fire and blew on the embers to get the fire going again. As the soot and smoke blew back into his eyes, he saw a figure come through the doorway.

"Good morning," Lirra said as she walked into the roundhouse. She had a small basket filled with bread. "You had no food," she said as she put the basket down on one of the beds.

"I've been at the broch for a month," Cador said, using the Latin word for month. He realized his mistake as Lirra stared at him blankly. "Since the new moon," he corrected himself.

"Your uncle lives off of ale," Lirra said with disdain, "that is what my Da says. So, he kept no food here." Lirra nodded, she was satisfied with that explanation.

"I'm afraid that's true," Cador said. He stood and walked over to the bed with that held the basket of bread. He was not ready for married life, he had no table, no food, he had lived a very simple life. "I can hunt for some meat this afternoon," Cador added, hoping for Lirra's approval.

"Meat would be good," Lirra said, she handed Cador some bread and took some for herself. They broke the loaves open and ate. Standing by the bed. The fire was warming up the room and making it feel more like a home.

"Lirra," Cador said, "I was not expecting to be married yesterday." Lirra looked at him and suddenly laughed.

"We were both forced into this?" Lirra asked. "You have wanted me since we first met, your eyes don't lie."

"You are a beautiful woman," Cador said honestly, "I'm certain most men would want you for your beauty."

"Thank you," Lirra said cautiously.

"I see more to you than beauty," Cador said carefully, "you don't feel like you need a man. Many girls I have met talk about getting married and having children. My sister was always talking about starting a family. You don't seem to care about that." Lirra's expression changed, she was amazed this giant of a man had seen that in her.

"It's not that I don't want a family," Lirra said, "I don't trust men." Lirra sat down on the bed and looked up at Cador. He stood so tall his head almost brushed the thatched roof of the house. "What you did for me last night," she took a deep breath, "by not forcing yourself on me." Cador could see she was struggling with some real emotional conflict. She couldn't finish her sentence. Cador got down on his knees so he could look Lirra in the eyes.

"You are my wife now," Cador said, "if we planned it this way or not, it has happened. That means that if you are hurt, so am I. I could not ask you to do anything you didn't want to do." Lirra put a hand on his cheek and smiled sadly at him.

"Will you always be this good to me?" Lirra asked softly.

"I hope I am," Cador said. They stayed like that for a minute; Cador could feel pain in his knees but didn't move as Lirra kept a hand on him. Any touch from her made him feel special. Finally, Lirra sighed and stood up. Cador got up with her as she looked around the roundhouse.

"My father has promised a cow," Lirra said firmly. "Maybe we can trade it for a table and some food. We need to find a way to make this place a better home. I refuse to live like a man." Cador laughed and walked over to the fire to put another log on.

"I will talk to Galan," Cador said, "maybe he will trade my young cow for one that is giving milk." Lirra smiled, a real smile.

"Good," Lirra said. "You get some meat and I will start making this place into a home. Tonight, we will feast on the meat you bring home and have our own celebration." Cador quickly put

on his cloak and took his spear out to see what he
could find for the celebration.

As he walked, Cador thought back to the
conversation with Lirra. He wondered what it was
that she wasn't telling him. He wondered what had
caused her to lose her trust in men. He found a
densely wooded area and using some of the tall
grass he fashioned a rope and set several snares
close to some berry plants.

He also gathered some of the berries and
put them into a small pouch he had on his belt. He
went further into the woods, as quietly as he could.
It was times like this Cador envied his brother's
small frame. It was hard to be quiet when you were
so large.

Cador found some rabbit tracks in the soft
soil and followed them slowly. Soon he saw the
animal that had left the prints, it was a good-sized
rabbit. Cador had a sling in his pouch, he was not a
good shot with it, but it was the better weapon for
killing a small animal. He picked up a smooth stone
that was close to him and put it in the leather
pocket of the sling. He pulled the leather thong of
the sling tight and started to swing the rock around.
If he wasn't surrounded by trees, he would have
been able to swing it fully, but he couldn't here. He
got a good swing on it and let go of the one strap,
sending the stone flying. It went past the rabbit, so
far above its head that the rabbit didn't even notice.

Letting out a silent oath, Cador looked for another stone. He couldn't find a smooth one and settled for a rough one. He placed it in the sling and tried to control the sling so he could improve his aim. He carefully released the stone, and it found its target. The rabbit startled and then fell dead. It was still twitching as Cador grabbed its back legs and picked it up. It wasn't big but would be a good meal for their celebration. He followed his trail back to the snares and found he had managed to catch a small grouse as well. The bird was still alive, so he wrung its neck. One of the other snares had broken, likely a large bird had managed to escape. Cador dismantled the remaining shares and started the walk home. It had been a good day hunting.

The sun was getting low as Cador approached the roundhouse. He could smell fresh bread coming from the house. There was a cow tied to a post outside his house and some chickens scratching at the ground by the entrance to his home. He walked in to find that Lirra had made the second bed into a table. She was putting some flowers into an clay pitcher. She smiled at him as he came in.

"Welcome home," Lirra said. Cador held up this catch from the day, and she gave him a look of appreciation. "That will make a good celebration! My father brought over the cow he promised and he added some chickens."

"You seem happy," Cador said.

"I have never really been able to do what I wanted with my day," Lirra said, "I felt so free." Cador wondered about what her life had been like before marrying him. He shook his head, she was happy, he didn't need to ruin that by saying anything. Lirra took the rabbit and grouse out to prepare them for dinner. Cador went out to collect some firewood, the supply inside was getting low.

They went through the various tasks to prepare their special meal together quietly. Cador had never been one for talking and realized that Lirra was the same. He was glad, he remembered once when spending time with his sister wondering if his future wife would talk so much. He kept looking over to her as they worked, expecting her to start talking about her day. She was just working contentedly. Finally, the rabbit and grouse were roasted and the fat from the grouse rendered to a sauce. It was a wonderful meal they had set before them, as they sat on the ground by the fire.

"You are a good cook," Cador said as he ate some of the bread dipped in the grouse fat.

"Thank you," Lirra smiled. "What was your life like before coming here?" Cador was a little taken aback by the question, it made sense they should get to know each other.

"I grew up in an inn near Caerwyn," Cador said, "my parents run it, they have accepted the Roman ways."

"That sounds hard," Lirra said, "did you know any Romans?"

"Many," Cador said.

"What are Romans like?" Lirra asked, shifting her weight so she was on her knees, she was really interested in what he was saying.

"They are people," Cador said, "some are nice and others are mean."

"Is it true that they are made and not born?" Lirra asked. "My Da said that the gods make them and they are not able to have children."

"I've never seen one born," Cador said, "but they have children. Druscilla was young when my mother started to care for her."

"Druscilla?" Lirra asked.

"A Roman girl my parents raised," Cador explained, "she's the other person that owns their inn."

"That's interesting," Lirra moved again so that she was sitting close to Cador. Their arms brushed and Lirra moved a little closer. Cador put an arm around her and she snuggled in close.

"What about you?" Cador asked, Lirra stiffened a little in his arms. "What is your favorite memory?"

"Spending time with my sisters," Lirra said. "We used to sit and make up stories about monsters coming, and how we would defeat them." Lirra laughed, noticeably relaxing in Cador's arms. Cador laughed as well, letting her relax into his embrace.

They sat there in silence for a long time. Cador thought back to a conversation he had with his father when he was younger. He had noticed that his parents would sit by the fire in the courtyard without talking. He asked his father why they didn't talk. His father explained that sometimes when you love someone, just sitting next to them is all you need. Cador had dismissed that as craziness, but right now, holding Lirra in his arms, he realized it was true.

Lirra leaned back and put her head on Cador's shoulder. As he turned to her, she put a hand behind his neck, stretched around and kissed him. He wasn't sure what to think, he just enjoyed the kiss. The feel of her lips, pressing firmly against his. She was strong and confident; he could feel it in her kiss. She pulled back and put her head on his shoulder.

Lirra giggled a little as they sat there basking in the afterglow of the kiss. Cador could feel a passion for her growing deep inside of him. While he would not force himself on her, the desire was growing. Lirra put a hand on his chest, surely, she

could feel his heart beating. She sat up and looked
at him, the firelight behind her emphasizing her
beauty. Lirra stood up and put out a hand for
Cador. He gave her a hand and she pulled him up.
She pulled him over to the bed.

Chapter 18

Maeli took Druscilla's crate out of the old villa back to the wagon. The man who had bought the land from Druscilla had offered her a week at his domus back in Roma while she got her affairs in order. This man was a friend of Titus Aelus and wanted to help Druscilla in this small way.

When they arrived at the domus, Druscilla went to work making arrangements for passage to Londinium. Maeli followed her around the city, visiting various companies that offered passage. They all wanted a lot of money, but finally she found one they could afford. They would be able to use a raeda, a hired wagon to travel to the harbor. A merchant ship would give them a single berth to cross the sea. This would leave them in Gaul and not Brittania, but Druscilla hoped to arrange the final leg from there.

Maeli wasn't sure how she would ride if they had one berth for Druscilla. On the way from Rome, they had a private boat, and she slept out on the deck in Druscilla's berth. Some of the slaves slept on the open deck. They told her it was cold and wet. She imagined this would be her fate for the journey home. Druscilla counted out the coins left in her purse and beckoned Maeli.

"We have one more important stop and then home to pack," Druscilla said swiftly. Maeli followed her along the road until they arrived at the same large building where that man had taken away everything Druscilla owned. More precisely everything Titus had owned. They walked into the same cave like room where the same fat man sat on the chair.

Josephus was already there, sent on ahead with some documents. He joined them and stood with Maeli behind Druscilla. They were called to stand before the magistrate.

"I have a petition for a maumissio vindicta," the man said. Maeli could not follow the big words but didn't dare ask for translation in this stern place. "Josephus of Judea come forward," the man said. Josephus obeyed and the man pulled a staff from his table. It wasn't long, but it was as thick as a finger. Maeli hoped she wouldn't have to watch her friend be beaten. The man gently touched Josephus' shoulder with the stick.

"I grant you freedom," Druscilla said. Maeli put her hands to her mouth, what a nice gift to give the man. Josephus had been a wonderful servant and helper. It made sense to Maeli that Druscilla reward his years of service. Then the man then called Maeli up to the stand. She walked past Druscilla who was looking ahead, a small smile pressing at the corners of her lips.

The fat man looked at her, he seemed concerned. "She's a bit young," the fat man said.

Maeli's spirit dropped. They wouldn't make her free because she was so young. Then Titus' friend who had shared his domus stepped forward.

"If it pleases the magistrate," the friend said, "the emperor had taken Domina Druscilla's husband and her home, leave her the dignity of one last request before she leaves Roma in disgrace." The fat man shook his head and frowned but lay the staff on Maeli's shoulder.

"You are free," Druscilla said. Maeli felt such joy bubbling inside her. She was no longer a slave. They couldn't tell her she had to stay in this forsaken city. She was free!

Maeli managed to walk slowly back to Druscilla. She took her spot behind Druscilla and followed her out past the pillars and into the street. Druscilla put both hands out and Josephus took one while Maeli took the other. The three friends returned to the domus walking hand in hand.

Back in the atrium Druscilla took Josephus aside. Maeli wondered what the man would do now that he was free. The two had a serious conversation and Druscilla came back to Maeli.

"Thank you," Maeli said, she had thought of so many things to say on the way home and this was all she could manage.

"Maeli," Druscilla said, "I want to ask one thing of you, please stay with me. I have no children, and now I know I will not have any. You have impressed me while living with me. I wish you were my daughter." Druscilla had tears flowing down her face, she knew she wasn't saying everything she felt, but she was trying.

"You have treated me better than I expected," Maeli said. She was starting to choke up as well. "I will stay with you; I have nowhere else to go. You are the closest thing to family I have now." She started to cry, feeling the loss of her family at this moment. She knew deep down what Druscilla was feeling. The two women embraced each other and stood in the atrium for a long time just holding each other.

Maeli thought back to her own mother, she had been a strong woman. When raiders had attacked their village she fought them off with a knife. She defended Maeli with her own life. Right now, she understood again the love her mother had for her. In an odd way she felt it from her old Domina. Josephus finally interrupted the ladies, encouraging them to finish getting everything together for the trip to Brittania.

"You're coming?" Maeli said, a little confused.

"Of course I am," Josephus said with a smile. "I much prefer Brittania, maybe one day I will head back to Judea, but you are not rid of me yet."

"I have something for you," Druscilla said as they got to the small cubiculum. She brought out a small box that Maeli recognized immediately. She knew it held a gold broach with a green gemstone in the middle. She had often admired it as she helped Druscilla pin it on. "This is yours," Druscilla said, handing it over.

"You don't have to," Maeli said shyly.

"No, I don't," Druscilla said, "it suits you, and once we get to Brittania I want you to wear it. You need to look like my daughter, not a slave." Maeli pinned it to her cloak and looked down at it, the light from the torch shimmered off it in the most beautiful way.

The next day they loaded into the raeda, it was small and a little cramped, but the three of them managed to get their belongings in as well as themselves. The trip was long and dusty, but it didn't bother Maeli, she was headed home. In the evenings they stayed at cauponae on the road. Maeli couldn't believe how poorly run they were compared to Aedan's caupona.

It was at one of these cauponae that Maeli had a realization. She was thinking about Aedan and that night when they kissed. She wondered if he had married in her mind, she had a hard time imagining him married. She came up with a plan for what to do if he was still not married when they arrived. If he was, all was lost. As they sat in the wagon the next morning, she turned to Druscilla.

"Do you remember Aedan?" Maeli asked hopefully.

"Of course I do," Druscilla said with a laugh.

"I think I'm in love with him," Maeli said quietly. Druscilla let out a little squeal of delight.

"That is wonderful!" Druscilla said. "Imagine if the two of you were married. That would be amazing!"

"That won't happen," Maeli said softly, "he's betrothed."

"Betrothals are just politics my dear," Druscilla said, "if he's not already married, that is easily remedied. I've been the wife of a politician long enough to know how to fix that." Maeli smiled and sat back in her seat. She had hoped that Druscilla would react this way.

Chapter 19

Aedan and Owain lifted the wooden sign with the symbol of the triskelion and placed on the hook by the arched entrance to the caupona. This would let everyone know they were receiving guests. Seren stood on the road and watched the two working hard. Owain's muscles rippled as he shifted the sign a little higher. Seren liked watching Owain working, he had a rugged face. His face was a little wider than her brother's and when he smiled it seemed to take up his whole face.

"Looks good," Seren said to the men, they thought she meant the sign. Seren walked past, taking one last look at Owain as she went through the arch into the courtyard. Her father had woken up earlier that day but was still weak. She had helped her mother take him up the stairs to his own bed before changing the linens in the guest room and washing them. They were hanging on a line in the stables; Seren went to check to see if they were dry.

The cow was lowing in its stall, probably wanting more grain. Seren walked over to check the trough, and it was empty. She was about to get the bucket to give it more grain when Owain entered the stable.

"She wants grass," Owain said, he had grown up around cows and had offered to take care

136

of their cow until Corin was feeling better. Owain whispered something to the cow, and it followed him out of the stables into the courtyard. Seren watched in awe, that cow was stubborn, it did not obey anyone. Here it was willingly following Owain. She laughed at herself at the thought that she probably would have done the same for him.

After removing the dry linens from the line, Seren went up to her parent's room to check on her father. He was still lying in bed, the medicus had not managed to balance his humors.

"Do you need anything Da?" Seren asked cheerfully.

"I need to get to work," Corin said, "but I'm just not able to stand for a minute without feeling like everything is spinning."

"Owain is helping," Seren said, sitting on the edge of her father's bed. "He's coming over each day."

"Your Ma told me," Corin said. "I've been thinking, we need to make sure your future is set. In all this I haven't managed to set your betrothal." It was like her father to think of her when he was so sick.

"Yes," Seren said, "I was thinking about that."

"Were you?" Corin said with a laugh that led to a coughing fit. Once the coughing stopped, he continued, "did you have anyone in mind?"

Seren suspected that her father already knew what was in her heart, he had always seemed to know what she was thinking.

"Owain is not promised," Seren said. Seren was trying not to sound desperate; he was the only one in her mind. Corin laid a hand on hers and smiled.

"Good," Corin said, "I've already sent word to his family, they will be over this afternoon." Seren jumped up in excitement. She hugged him and rushed off to get herself cleaned up for Owain's family. After a trip to the bathhouse, Seren got herself dressed in her nicest clothes. She hoped that Owain wanted her to be his wife. As she was about to head down the stairs, she saw her father standing in the entrance to his room.

"Can you help me down the stairs?" Corin asked. "I want to wait in the courtyard for Owain's father." Seren took her father's arm and guided him to the stairs. They slowly made their way to the courtyard, where Corin sat by the fire Aedan had built to keep him warm. He sat in a chair, looking a little more like himself in the sunlight.

When Owain's parents arrived, Seren waited in the kitchen, watching nervously. Her father and Owain's father seemed to be talking forever. She tried to read their faces to decide if the conversation was going well. As she was sitting there Aedan came up behind her.

"What's going on?" Aedan asked, startling Seren.

"Why are you sneaking up on me?" Seren asked.

"I wasn't sneaking," Aedan said, "you were so focused on them, you didn't hear me."

"They are trying to arrange a marriage," Seren said. "Do they look like things are going well?" Aedan laughed at his sister.

"Want me to spy on them?" Aedan asked.

"No!" Seren said, "I don't think we need to do that." Aedan chuckled as he sat next to his sister.

"It looks like they are happy," Aedan said, "they have always gotten along. Your marriage would help both families. Owain obviously likes you. He doesn't really need to come here every day." Seren blushed a little and pushed her brother's shoulder. The men stood and walked over to the kitchen. Seren held her breath as they came over.

The men went to the barrel in the back of the kitchen and Corin poured them each an ale. They drank together, which Seren took to be a good sign. An agreement was made. Corin told Aedan to fetch Owain, which assured Seren it was good news.

Corin called Eira over from the table where she was standing, talking with Owain's mother.

Seren had been so focused on the men she hadn't noticed them there. They all sat around the table with expectation. Aedan returned with Owain and they sat with the group.

"I'm not going to keep everyone waiting," Corin said, "we have made an agreement for the betrothal of Owain and Seren." Seren felt her heart leap in her chest. She was going to marry Owain. There was a round of congratulations from everyone at the table. Owain stood at his spot, and everyone turned to him.

"This is good news," Owain said, his smile lighting up his face. "Seren, I promise to be a good husband to you. May the gods bless this decision." Owain lifted his cup and drank his ale.

"The inn is open, and we have a betrothal," Eira said, "I think this calls for a celebration!"

"That is a wonderful idea," Corin said, "we can let the people of Caerwyn know we will have a feast here tomorrow night!" The next while was spent planning for the feast and finally everyone decided they needed to get on with the day. Owain's parents left, cheerful about all that had been decided. As Owain went to the field to bring the cow home for milking, Seren stopped him in the arch.

"Are you really happy to by marrying me?" Seren asked. Owain looked into her pleading blue eyes and again gave that big smile.

"Seren," Owain said, "I've been waiting for you." Seren watched as he walked away, longing for them to be together. She prayed to the gods it would be soon.

The next day Corin seemed to make a miraculous recovery as he helped prepare for the feast. Aedan had gone out early in the morning and returned with a boar he had purchased from a poacher. They had dressed it and put it over the fire to cook slowly. The pan under it to catch the fat was soon spitting as the fat landed in it. Seren caught her brother's hand as he rushed through the kitchen.

"I can't help but feel bad," Seren said, "after you've lost Caela, celebrating my betrothal."

"Don't feel bad," Aedan said, "I'm happy for you and Owain. He's a good man." Aedan started to walk away, then turned back, "he's not worthy of you, of course, but he'll have to do." Seren laughed as she watched her brother join the group of men moving tables in the courtyard. Corin was supervising, arranging the tables around the herbs and other plants in the courtyard.

The boar was starting to smell good, and the other food was prepared as people arrived from the village. Seren was certain some had just come out of curiosity about the inn that had been closed by the Romans and suddenly opened again. The gossip about the assassination of the Senator has started up again. People did not understand why the inn had been released from all responsibility for the man's death.

As the people got comfortable, Aedan and Eira started to bring food to the tables. Seren sat with Owain at one table, and people came over to congratulate the two. Seren was beaming with the attention, as the innkeeper's daughter she had never really been seen as important.

Owain's family had a number of cows and supplied most of the village with butter and cheese. They were respected in Caerwyn and a marriage between one of them and the daughter of the only innkeeper was seen as a natural pairing. Finally, the time was getting late and Corin stood with his hands raised to get everyone's attention. People quieted down to listen.

"After a year, we are happy to announce that the man responsible for the attack on the Senator has been found," Corin said. He sounded as if the Emperor himself had told him and he wasn't extracting all his information from the short declaration left on their door. "The Caupona Caureni will be open once more." This was met with some cheers of approval by the people.

"We are also happy that Owain and Seren will be married soon," Corin continued. "As many of you know…" suddenly Corin fell backwards and collapsed onto the ground. Eira let out a gasp as she jumped from her seat to his side. Aedan went to his father's side and lightly shook him, but he did not respond.

"I'll get the medicus," Aedan announced.

"Take my horse," someone in the crowd called out. Aedan went with that man to the post by the gate where a horse was tethered. Aedan thanked the man as he climbed up onto the horse. He had not ridden more than a few times in his life, but Aedan was sure he could manage the trip to the fort.

Owain and Seren helped Eira get Corin to a guest room. After Corin was settled, Owain went out to the crowd to assure them all would be well and that it might be best to let the family have some space. He then returned to Seren's side and put his arm around her to comfort her. Corin lay there unaware of anything going on around him.

Chapter 20

The men stood side by side on the hillside a good distance from the broch. When word had reached Galan that the river clan was coming, he called all his warriors together. Cador had rushed with Lirra to the broch, kissing her at the entrance to the tall grey tower before joining his comrades to defend the clan.

Cador watched as the men took their spears and started to hit their shields. The rhythm was to build excitement in the men and put fear into the hearts of the enemy. Cador didn't feel as much excitement as he did fear. He had been practicing with spear and sword this past week, he still didn't know that he was ready.

As the mist rose out of the valley, the sun barely cutting through the fog this cold morning, they heard the men coming. Cador understood in that moment that hearing your enemy without seeing them was a frightening thing. For a moment he wondered why he was here at all. He was raised to run an inn, not to fight battles.

Cador wondered what his family was up to right now. They would be preparing food for any guests who were about to leave. His mother would already have the bread cooking, and the smell would be making Aedan complain about being hungry. He would be helping Rian set the fire for the bathhouse and getting horses ready for guests.

Galan let out a battle cry, he was a small man but he could make himself heard across the hills. The other men took up the yell and rushed forwards down the hill. Cador joined in, trying to sound fearsome as he ran with the others towards an enemy he had not seen yet.

As they were enveloped by the fog, the inn, his family, even Lirra up at the Broch felt like it was part of another world. Cador could hear the men around him but still felt alone. Then he saw the enemy! A couple of men ahead of him running in his direction.

Cador slowed down and positioned his spear so that it was in front of him. It wasn't long before the spear connected with the shield of one of the men. Cador had not been prepared for the shock running through the spear and almost dropped it. He saw a flash of movement coming towards his head and raised his shield in time to block it.

Cador turned to face the man that had attacked him, his shield up. He felt the other man's shield crash against his shield and thrust his spear forward. It came into contact with something and he heard the awful sound of a man crying out in pain. Cador pulled back his spear as the pressure against his shield fell away. He had won this fight quickly but still had more to go.

Another shield was visible ahead, and it was not painted with the emblem of the boar, so it belonged to the enemy. Galan had drilled that into him, look for the boar, don't kill the boar. He raised his shield and crashed into the enemy. The other man lost his footing and fell to the ground, Cador landing on top of him. He could feel the firm body underneath him and scrambled to get up again. He saw the sword before it connected with his war-coat. The sword was deflected by the thick leather.

Cador tried to reach the hilt of his own sword but couldn't find it. The man he had landed on was trying to wrap his legs around Cador to make him stop moving. Cador pushed up against his shield and felt something beneath him crack. The man beneath him pushed Cador off as roughly as he could. Cador rolled off and found himself flat on his back, the man he had been atop of was rising over him.

Cador tried to raise his shield but found it was too heavy. He realized the man was standing on it. Finding his sword hilt, he pulled the sword out to defend himself when the man staggered away. The man was breathing heavily and looked wounded. Cador could not see a wound but took the opportunity to stand and face the man.

The man swung his sword at Cador which Cador easily knocked away with his shield. Now that they were face to face, Cador could see his long-braided beard and his helmet, decorated with the same symbol that was hanging above the inn door. Cador stared at the symbol for moment, before trying to thrust his sword at the man's face. It was deflected easily by the man.

Cador got ready for another attack when the man's expression changed from hatred to fear. Cador took this to mean he could win this fight too. He stepped back to give himself some momentum when the men fell to the ground and lay there gasping for air. Cador felt someone next to him and turned to attack when he saw the boar on the man's shield.

"Finish him off!" Bran shouted in Cador's ear. Cador had not realized Bran was here. Cador thrust his sword into the fallen man and then rushed on to find another enemy to fight. The woods in the valley were filled with men now. Dodging around trees, Cador moved between men who were fighting their own battles.

There was a boar shield on the ground, imbedded in the mud so that it stood upright. Corin rushed over and saw the distinct form of Galan lying on the ground. Another man stood over him about to impale him with a spear. Cador saw a spear laying on the ground close to him and rushed to it. He picked up the spear and realized he was too far to thrust, so he threw it with all his might. It went into the man's war-coat, slowed by the leather it punctured the man's side but did not kill him.

Suddenly wounded, the man turned to look at Cador. He was young, about the same age as Cador and almost as big. The man turned to face his new enemy. Galan scrambled to his feet behind the man, seemingly forgotten as the man faced a new threat. Cador pulled out his sword and charged the man, his shield in front of him. The two shields crashed loudly, some people around stopped fighting at the sight of the two big men fighting. Cador thrust his sword around the shield but hit nothing.

A sword came around his shield, but he parried it with his own sword. He braced himself and pushed, but the other man must have done the same thing. It was a stalemate between the two giants. Cador had the odd realization that people were watching them in awe, the biggest men from each side had found each other. It was a spectacular sight.

They started to circle each other, trying to gain an advantage. Each man trying to use his weight to push the other one away. Cador felt his foot come up against the root of a tree and remembered a story his father told him about fighting someone in a similar circumstance. Cador put his foot on the tree and pushed off with all his might. The other man lost his footing. Cador saw that the spear was still sticking out of the man's leather armor and used both arms to twist his shield as he straightened the leg against the tree.

The man fell and let out a loud scream as the spear caught between two rocks and the weight of the man pushed the spear into his side. He stumbled to get his feet under himself again and pulled at the spear. The man seemed to forget all about Cador, he had one enemy now, the spear. Cador drew his sword and thrust it into the man's side. As the blood flowed the members of his clan let out a cry of victory, Cador brought his sword back and watched as the men from the River Clan ran away, their morale defeated as they watched their champion die.

Galan grabbed Cador's arm and lifted it as high as he could. Their comrades gathered around them to cheer. They returned to the broch and Galan called ahead.

"Women! Prepare us a feast!" Galan shouted. "Māros Cador has won a great victory!" Cador laughed at the idea that he was a giant. He was taller than most men, but he never thought of himself as a giant. The women came cautiously out of the broch, Lirra first among them. She rushed to Cador and put her arms around his neck. He lifted her for a kiss, this had become their custom, so he didn't have to lean down, and she didn't have to crane her neck.

"Welcome home," Lirra said softly, "I've been waiting for you." Lirra ran a hand down Cador's back and then walked with him to the others. The men were demanding ale and food be brought out quickly. Cador felt like he was among the Romans at the inn, warriors were the same everywhere.

Barrels of ale appeared and tankards were handed around. Cador realized how hungry he was, he had not thought about it until he was handed a plate with stacks of cold meats, cheese and bread. Fires were then lit and the women started to prepare hot food.

Lirra was finally able to sit with Cador and enjoy the feast for a time. She put a hand on his thigh and squeezed, he looked around and noticed that nobody had seen this display of affection. He put his hand on hers and interlaced his fingers with hers. Lirra reached up and kissed his cheek before getting up to help with the food preparation again.

A new group started up the hill to the broch. Cador realized it was the old men and those who were too weak to fight carrying the dead back. One of the bodies was wearing a familiar cloak. Cador jumped up and rushed over to see if he was right in what he saw. It was Bran, looking like he was sleeping peacefully on the grass.

Bran was gone. The man that had encouraged him to fight against Roman oppression. The man that had brought him here. The man ultimately responsible for him finding Lirra. Gone.

Chapter 21

The worst part of the journey was behind them, and Maeli decided that she would never cross the sea again. The constant movement of the boat made both her and Druscilla sick. They had spent the entire journey laying on their bunks in the cabin. Josephus had been the son of a fisherman and loved the sea. He took care of the ladies and cleaned up after them. When they landed, Josephus announced he was going to stay with the ship.

"I didn't realize how much I missed it," Josephus told them. I will come to visit you at the Caupona Caureni." They shared a tearful goodbye and as Druscilla stepped away, Josephus put a small stack pf parchment, stitched together at one end to form a codex into Maeli's hands. "It's the letter from Paulus; I have rewritten it in Latin for you."

"I can't read," Maeli said.

"But your man can," Josephus said with a wink, "have him read it to you." With that he was gone. Maeli put the codex into a small satchel which held all her belongings. She joined Druscilla walking down the streets of Londinium. They had arranged transit from Gaul on a trading ship, but it had cost almost all the money Druscilla had left.

They found a small shop, almost hidden away between a public bathhouse and an insulae. It was a trader who dealt in fine wool and other furs.

As Druscilla and Maeli entered, the woman sitting in the shop's face lit up. Maeli recognized her but it took a moment to recall her name, she was called Tegwen. She had come from somewhere to the south. A widow who had come here to trade. She was knowledgeable about wool and furs and became popular among the wealthy.

"Druscilla!" Tegwen said, standing and limping over to the ladies. "I heard you were in Roma!"

"I came home," Druscilla said, "this is Maeli, you remember her?"

"That hair?" Tegwen said, "I could never forget you girl." The older woman walked over and patted Maeli on the head. "What can I help you with today? I have some wonderful fox furs, very warm as the winter comes in."

"Unfortunately," Druscilla said. "I'm short of sestertii now. My husband is gone and I'm left with nothing but my father's caupona."

"Goodness!" Tegwen said, she put a comforting hand on Druscilla's arm. "Tragedy makes us sisters. But then why did you come to me, I wonder? Ah! You knew I could help get you home. I know a young man who can help. He's walking that way; he can keep you company. Better to have good company from a young man than for two women to walk alone." Tegwen nodded her head sagely. She beckoned them to follow her. The walked down a back alley from behind the shop to a small caupona on close to the edge of town.

Tegwen led them into the courtyard where she spotted a handsome young man sitting at a table. They walked over to him, he had a smaller face, which almost made him look like a child. His dark hair played against his light complexion in a very becoming way.

"This is Iowerth," Tegwen said, "handsome isn't he?" She looked at Maeli who gave a polite smile. "His family home is close to your caupona, he can escort you. You will escort them? It would be a favor for me." Iowerth looked a little taken aback at the sudden request. He had been raised to always listen to his elders.

"Of course," Iowerth said, "always glad for company." If we leave first thing tomorrow, we can get there the day after. Maeli could tell the prospect of walking all that way didn't appeal to Druscilla. Maeli had to admit, living in a wealthy household had spoiled her as well.

"She has little money," Tegwen said.

"I can pay for what we need on the journey," Iowerth said with a smile. "I'm sure Corin and Eira will pay me back."

"You know who we are?" Maeli asked.

"I do," Iowerth said, "my cousin was betrothed to Aedan, I was often at the caupona, especially when free food was available." Maeli noticed he said she was betrothed to Aedan, like it was in the past. Had something happened to change that? She wanted to ask but didn't really know this stranger.

They spent the night at the small caupona and then left early the next morning. The further they got from Londinium, the fewer people they saw. The sun was bright but wasn't giving much heat. Winter was coming again, Iowerth explained that this walk was terrible in the middle of the summer weather. It was easier now because walking warmed you up. Maeli was impressed that this man was able to talk the entire day and say nothing that was important.

They spent the night at another caupona, this one was larger than Aedan's. It did take some time to get used to having a cubiculum and not staying in the slave's quarters. As they ate that evening, Druscilla asked for news from Caerwyn.

"The caupona has been shut down for a year now," Iowerth told them. "Suspicion about that Senator that was killed. That's when my uncle ended the betrothal with Aedan. I guess they think he did it, I don't know. He doesn't seem to be the type." It was brief but the good news was there, Aedan was no longer betrothed. Druscilla caught that too and gave Maeli a conspiratorial look. She would see Maeli and Aedan married yet.

"So, they haven't had guests for a year?" Maeli asked, trying to contain her excitement.

"I guess not," Iowerth said. "I just go into the field with my sheep. I don't follow what goes on in the village. I come to Londinium to sell wool, that's the most I want to get involved with anyone." Maeli wondered how he survived alone with his sheep, or how his sheep survived him talking all the time.

"I suppose we should sleep," Druscilla finally said. It's a long walk again tomorrow. Iowerth agreed and said goodnight. Druscilla and Maeli went to the cubiculum they would share.

"A year without guests," Druscilla said as she lay down. Maeli wondered what that would do to Aedan's family. She wasn't sure about running a caupona, but imagined it wasn't easy without guests.

"How do you think they are doing?" Maeli asked.

"I don't know," Druscilla said, "Eira was always careful with money, but a year is a long time. At least Aedan is free to marry you." Maeli had heard the worry in her friend's voice but recognized the need to talk about something a little less serious.

"I hope he'll have me," Maeli said.

"We will find out tomorrow," Druscilla said, Maeli could hear joy in her voice. She wasn't just thinking about Aedan's choice of wife. She had lost everyone but these two innkeepers, she needed them now.

After a fitful sleep, Maeli was still not used to padded bedding, they headed out for Caerwyn. Iowerth said if they made good time they should arrive by midafternoon. Energized by the thought of finally finishing the journey, they walked with enthusiasm. Iowerth telling them all about his sheep the whole way.

When the inn came into sight, both women breathed a sigh of relief. They could stop walking and they could stop hearing about the daily life of sheep. The big arched entrance stood there as solid as ever, with the sign of the triskelion hanging from it.

"That's odd," Iowerth said, "the legionaries are gone." Druscilla wondered if that meant that Titus' sacrifice had cleared them of all suspicion. It made sense, if Titus claimed all responsibility, the senate would not see the need to hold anyone else accountable. They quickened their pace a little and got to the archway and Druscilla's countenance changed, she was home.

The courtyard was eerily quiet, there were no slaves moving around, no guests sitting at the tables. Druscilla worried about what was going on. She walked into the kitchen and the fire in the big hearth was down to embers. Was anyone here, she wondered. Maeli followed Druscilla to the stairs and up to where the family all lived. She knocked lightly on the door.

The door opened and Seren looked out, her blond hair was matted and her face was red, like she had been crying. When she saw Druscilla, her face lit up.

"Ma, it's Druscilla!" Seren called out. There was the sound of movement and Eira came to the door, in a similar state to her daughter.

"What's wrong?" Druscilla asked.

"Corin has a fever," Eira said, "he's not likely to last much longer."

"By the gods!" Druscilla replied, "can I see him?" Eira led Druscilla to the small bed where Corin was laying. He was asleep and his body was covered in sweat. Druscilla knelt next to the bed and took his hand. "Da, I'm here," she whispered. She didn't know why she called him "Da," but it felt right in the moment.

Maeli took a step back into the large room where Seren and Aedan were sitting on their beds. Aedan looked lost, stuck in his own head. Maeli longed to hold him, but he hadn't even realized she was here.

"Aedan," Seren said, coming up behind Maeli, "you have a guest." Aedan looked over and for a moment didn't seem to recognize Maeli. He then stood up quickly and rushed to her. He grabbed her hands gently and looked into her eyes.

"Are you really here?" Aedan asked.

"Yes," Maeli said, feeling her emotions welling up inside of her. "I am." Aedan wrapped his arms around Maeli and held her. Maeli held Aedan tight, never wanting to let go again.

In the other room, Corin's eyes slowly opened and he saw Druscilla by the side of his bed. She had her head down, obviously crying for him. He put his hand on her head.

"Is that really Druscilla?" Corin asked, "the Domina amicila?" Corin used his term of endearment for the little mistress. Druscilla smiled.

"I'm here," Druscilla said, "home to help you get well again."

"My family is almost whole," Corin said quietly. Druscilla looked over at Eira, confused.

"Cador is still missing," Eira explained. "We don't know where he has gone."

"I'll find him," Druscilla promised, "I'll bring him home." Corin took her hand. Druscilla worked as hard as she could to keep her emotions under control.

"When you do," Corin said, "tell him I don't blame him for what happened." He called for Eira who came to his side and Druscilla stepped out of the room to get the others. She sensed that Corin knew his time was close. As they came back into the room. Corin was holding Eira's hand and staring into her eyes.

"I love you," Corin was saying, "I will always love you." Corin took a shallow breath and looked out at his children. "Seren," he reached out to his daughter. She stepped forward and sat on the bed next to her father.

"Yes Da," Seren said.

"You make sure you take care of your mother and brother," Corin said, "they need to be reminded to enjoy life."

"Of course, Da," Seren said, a single tear fell down her cheek.

"Aedan," Corin called out. Aedan came and put his hand on Seren's shoulder, reaching down with his other to touch his father's arm. "I'm sorry in all this that's happened," Corin took another breath, it was getting more difficult. "I'm sorry you lost Caela for a wife." Another shallow breath. "I see you have found your girl with the hair of fire." Corin took another breath. He couldn't get enough air to finish his thought and closed his eyes.

"No," Eira said softly. Corin took another shallow breath and then stopped breathing.

Chapter 22

"Are you alright?" Lirra asked Cador. They were cuddled under the blanket; the sun was just coming up and except for the glowing embers in the fire the roundhouse was still dark. Cador was usually up and moving at this point, and Lirra was a little worried about him.

"Just feeling a little sad," Cador said, "Bran was my kin."

"He died with honor," Lirra said, putting her hand on Cador's chest and gently rubbing his muscles. "He's in the otherworld now, with your ancestors."

"He is," Cador said, enjoying the physical touch from his wife. He kissed her and snuggled in close. "I'm also afraid to go put a log on the fire, I might not get back without freezing to death!"

"Well then," Lirra laughed, "you better stay with me." She had discovered a few days back that he had a ticklish spot on his side and reached down and tickled him. He jumped and grabbed her hand; he leapt up and held her hand down while kneeling over her. Her expression changed from joy to fear in a second. Cador released her and moved back to lay beside her.

"Are you alright?" Cador asked. Lirra let out a sigh and got out of bed. She went to the fire and started stirring the coals with a stick, adding more wood so it would blaze up. "Lirra?" Cador called. Lirra sat by the fire and stared into the flames. Cador got out of bed and joined her.

"I'm sorry," Lirra said softly.

"What happened?" Cador said.

"You scared me," Lirra said. She took a deep breath and turned to Cador. "I know you didn't mean to," she said, "it took me back."

"What happened?" Cador asked.

"My father used to get angry sometimes," Lirra said, "he would hold me down and beat me." She shivered and laid her head on Cador's shoulder. "He never let me do anything I wanted, I don't know, maybe he hated me for something." Cador kissed the top of her head.

"I don't know why anyone would hate you," Cador said. "You are perfect." Lirra smiled. She was still staring into the fire, the flames playing across her pale face. Cador took in her straight nose and firm jawline. She was the perfect woman.

"That first night," Lirra seemed transfixed on the flames as she talked, "you didn't hurt me, you didn't make me do what I didn't want to do. I realized you were not the same as my Da." She put a hand on Cador's thigh, rubbing up and down in a tantalizing way. Cador smiled, his wife might have some issues, but she was a passionate woman.

It wasn't until the sun was high that Cador made it out of the roundhouse. He spent some time feeding and milking the cow and feeding the chickens before heading to the broch. Galan had sent word that he wanted Cador to join a raiding party.

When he arrived, there were already about twenty men gathered, spears and shields ready for the raid. Cador took his place among the men. Galan came out of his roundhouse and stood on a rock to make himself easier to see. The men grew silent.

"Men!" Galan shouted, "the Wolf Clan have taken two of my cows and killed my slave! We will go and get our revenge!" The men cheered and Galan stepped down to lead them on the march to the Wolf Clan's territory.

Cador wondered how much of his life would be dedicated to fighting. He liked being recognized as a warrior. He hated the actual fighting. Galan obviously enjoyed it, if he wasn't fighting, he was talking about it.

The walk was long and Cador could feel the tension grow the longer it went. He finally stopped thinking about the fight and let his mind go back to the morning with Lirra. He wondered why her father had been so rough with her. She was a good wife; always made sure he had what he needed. Cador wondered if that was a result of how she was brought up.

He thought maybe that in order to raise a girl to be a good wife you needed to be strict. Some women were strong willed and needed to be kept in their place. He had been swatted as a child and that had taught him to respect his father. Seren had never really needed to be punished, as far as he remembered. She was always respectful of men. Cador wondered how it would be best to raise his own children.

The sound of warriors beating their shields could be heard in the distance. Cador got a firm grip on his spear and focused on what he needed to do. He was the champion now, the one the others looked to when they saw the enemy. He could defeat the biggest and strongest.

Cador took in a deep breath as the sound got closer and then the woods they were walking through ended and they were in a field. Ahead of them was a ragged line of men carrying shields with wolves painted on them. There was no fog today, they could see each other clearly. The two groups of warriors started to run towards each other. The sound of the battle cries filling the air. Cador added his own cry as he rushed to the enemy.

As he approached the wolf clan, Cador thrust his spear into first man he saw. The man deflected it with his shield and ran past. Cador was about to turn when he saw a spear coming for him. He got his shield up in time to block the spear.

Cador turned to face his new opponent, using his shield to push at the man.

Their two shields crashed together, and Cador was thrown off balance. He rushed to regain his footing and tried to push back. He was low and off balance, so he decided to fall back onto the ground. Using his spear to direct his fall, he fell to the right causing the other man to lose his balance and fall forward. Cador heard laughing as he brought the edge of his shield down on the man, catching him on the jaw. As the man went limp, Cador realized he was the one laughing.

He scrambled to his feet, looking for the next man to take on the giant! Confidence in himself swelled as two men saw him and avoided him. He stood to his full height and lifted his spear over his head.

"I am Māros Cador," he yelled, "cower before me!" He looked at the men around him and no one had noticed. A little embarrassed, Cador turned to look for someone to fight. Somehow, he had gotten onto the far side of the fighting, he was alone on the enemy's side.

Galan was close by and Cador rushed over and with a quick thrust of a spear took down the man Galan was fighting.

"Follow me!" Cador shouted and rushed towards where he had been standing before. Using their spears they helped others win their individual battles and soon five men stood panting on the far end of the fighting. They had arrived unnoticed by anyone from the wolf clan.

"To the broch!" Galan said, and the five men followed him as they swiftly moved to the stone tower the wolf clan had built. As they approached, they were met by two older men, left behind the guard the women. Cador and another man squared off with the men while the others pushed through.

Cador used his shield to push the older warrior aside and realized quickly this was not a weak man. The older man pushed back, and Cador saw a sword come around the shield. It was too late for him to deflect the sword, and it pierced his side at a spot uncovered by his war coat. Cador felt the stab of pain and was enraged. He put all his weight behind his shield and pushed forward. The other man stumbled backwards.

Cador thrust his spear around his shield and felt it connect with the man's helmet. This stunned the man and he fell to the ground. Cador raised his spear and was about to bring it down when he heard women screaming. Galan was coming out of the broch with the other men. They were dragging a group of women and children behind them. Someone had managed to tie them up, but they were yelling and fighting back.

While Cador was distracted his opponent got back onto his feet. Cador swiftly thrust his spear in the man's side, killing him. He rushed to join the group that was taking the women. Galan grabbed one of the men close to him, a man that Cador knew was a trusted friend of Galan.

"Go!" Galan told the man, "call a retreat and meet back in the woods. We have what we came for!" The man rushed off, Galan told the other men to follow him. Cador fell in behind the group. Some of the men threatened to kill the women if they made any noise and the quieted down and followed meekly. Cador realized that this raid was to get the clan more slaves. He followed along quietly, thinking about stories his father had shared about being captured and enslaved.

Chapter 23

Corin was buried in a mound close to the caupona. After the burial, the family stood quietly by the mound to say their final goodbyes. He had been buried with his spear, although he had spent most of his life caring for others, he was still a warrior. He would be free to fight when needed in the other world.

Aedan held on to Seren's hand as they walked back to the caupona. They were determined to stay strong for their mother but were leaning on each other to get from day to day.

"You are the master of the caupona now," Seren said softly. "Have you thought about how we can run it?"

"I have," Aedan said, "I don't like keeping people. We will have no slaves." Seren stopped walking and turned to face her brother.

"How will we manage?" Seren asked.

"We will pay people," Aedan said, "if I increase the price of a stay by a few asses a night, I think we can pay."

"Owain says he wants to build our house close to the inn," Seren said, "we have a few years before marriage, but he wants to be a part of the caupona. He's enjoyed helping."

"He is welcome," Aedan said.

"What about Maeli?" Seren asked. Aedan looked back to where Maeli was walking with Druscilla and his mother.

"She's free now," Aedan said, "I will ask her to stay, but I can't make her stay." Seren stopped walking and looked back at the three women.

"She will stay," Seren said with a smile. Aedan pulled his sister along and the two walked silently for a while. Aedan wondered what Maeli would do. They hadn't had a moment to talk since she returned. She had been willing to help with getting his father prepared for burial, but Aedan didn't know her plans after that.

When Druscilla had told him she had been given her freedom, Aedan had dared to hope she had come for him. He also realized that coming with Druscilla had been her best chance of getting back to her own people. He just couldn't bear letting himself hope that she wanted him.

As they walked through the archway into the caupona courtyard, Aedan felt the weight of all that had happened fall onto his shoulders. The had little money left, no help and the caupona was in disarray. He would allow himself a day to finish mourning and get to business tomorrow.

As the sun set, the family gathered around the fire and shared their favorite memories of Corin. Eira shared how on the trip to Roma as slaves, Corin would try to keep her spirits up. They would tell jokes about the Romani men on the ship or find other ways to make each other laugh.

Druscilla talked about learning from Corin that everyone should be treated well, regardless of stature. While the inn kept slaves, they were always treated more like servants than slaves. She mentioned that once she had seen him forgive Hilarus for burning a hog he had been cooking. Most men would have beat a slave for such an expensive mistake.

Aedan shared how his father had always encouraged him in learning how to manage the money for the inn. Aedan had not been big and strong like his father or brother, but sums and writing came easy to him. His father told him he didn't need to be a warrior to be a man.

Seren talked of his patience and gentle spirit. She had heard stories of him killing men but never believed he could. He never seemed to get angry or want to hurt anyone.

"I saw him angry once," Druscilla said with a laugh. "Ten men came to kill me and only he and your mother stood between us. He took on all ten men!" Eira smiled at the memory.

"The only thing that would make him angry is if someone wanted to hurt one of us," Eira said.

"Or the sheep," Druscilla said with a smile, "he once told me he wrung the neck of a wolf that was attacking his sheep. Thinking back, he might have made that up." The whole family laughed. It felt weird to be laughing, but for a moment they could sense he was in the other world, watching them. Soon they were all ready for sleep. Eira, Seren and Aedan went up the stairs and Druscilla went to a guest cubiculum.

When morning came, Aedan asked everyone to meet him in the kitchen. He had built up a nice fire and had the area warmed up nicely by the time everyone arrived. Maeli came out of her cubiculum and Aedan called her to join them. Once they were all seated with a loaf of bread and some cheeses that Seren had put out, Aedan stood at the head of the table.

"I know we are all mourning," Aedan stated, "but I don't think Da would want to see the inn fail. We need to make plans." There was a sense of agreement around the table.

"First," Druscilla said, "let me tell you I have five hundred denarii left from selling my villa. I wish to see it invested in the inn." Aedan did some quick calculations in his head, that was enough to run the inn for several months, if he was careful.

"We can't ask you to do that," Eira said.

"I'm part owner of this caupona," Druscilla said somewhat sternly, "and it is the only thing of value I have left. If it fails, I have nothing."

"Thank you," Aedan said. "That solves a lot of our problems. Next, we need to figure out who will manage various tasks. The four of us cannot do everything."

"I will be staying to help," Maeli said, then added softly, "if you will let me."

"Of course," Eira said. "You are welcome."

"Owain is willing to help," Seren added.

"Owain?" Druscilla asked. In all the confusion, proper introductions had not been made.

"My betrothed," Seren said.

"I see," Druscilla looked over at Maeli and winked. "Aedan, what about your betrothed? That girl I met a few years ago."

"Her father broke the betrothal," Eira said gently.

"Oh no!" Druscilla said. "I know this isn't the way to do things, but as we are all family here. I think Maeli and Aedan would be a good match." There was a moment of stunned silence as every eye went to Druscilla. She just sat there as if this was a normal thing to say.

"I'm not sure," Eira said and paused in thought, "that isn't how to do things. I suppose since Maeli is an orphan and I'm the only parent involved." Eira took a deep breath and looked at the two. She suddenly realized they both were looking at her with a longing. "How do you feel about that Maeli?"

"I would like to marry Aedan," Maeli said, looking down at the table. She felt very self-conscious saying it out loud.

"Really?" Aedan blurted out. His expression told Eira all she needed to know.

"By the look on my son's face it's a match," Eira said. "You two are betrothed. How old are you child?"

"This is my seventeenth winter," Maeli said. Druscilla smiled, she had tried to get Maeli to use the proper Romani way of telling the years, but she never understood it well.

"Then you are old enough to marry," Eira said. "If you will be living with us, it would be best if it was soon." Aedan stifled a cheer; he thanked his mother and tried to get down to business. The discussion about hiring men for the stable and a cook to help in the kitchen, just didn't feel real anymore.

Maeli tried to follow the conversation, now that she would be married to Aedan the caupona's business would affect her. She couldn't get that thought out of her mind. She would be married to Aedan. She watched him as he discussed hiring men instead of buying more slaves. She was proud that he wanted to allow people their freedom.

The next few days were busy as they worked hard to clean up the courtyard, with Druscilla's money the garden could be removed. Owain and Aedan did most of the work, but they hired someone to lay the stones to make the courtyard more comfortable. Maeli helped Eira organize the kitchen, while Druscilla and Seren cleaned the guest quarters.

One day, Eira announced that she had made all the plans for the marriage to take place. They would do it properly, at the full moon near the river. This would help ensure that the gods would bless them with many children. Eira had been married in a cramped slave quarters in Roma. She wanted better for her children.

When the day came, Druscilla came to the cubiculum they had set aside for Maeli until she was married. Druscilla had moved up to the family residence, sharing a room with Eira. She brought a cloak she had purchased. It was beautiful green wool with white wool trim.

"This is beautiful," Maeli said, putting on the cloak. It would be cold by the river, but Eira was right, it was proper to perform the ceremony during the full moon at the river.

"I'm so happy Aedan brought you to me," Druscilla said, "you have become like a daughter. Your strength is inspiring."

"Thank you," Maeli said, looking at the cloak. "Ma." She added and looked in time to see Druscilla's face light up with joy.

"Come," Druscilla said, "we must get to the river." They walked out and took the path to the river where Aedan and his family were waiting. The ceremony was blessedly fast as their hands were bound together and they swore an oath to each other. Several people from the village had come to bear witness to their marriage and make it official.

They were so cold once they got back to the caupona, Aedan built up the fire in the courtyard to warm up the area. As they stood around it to warm up, Aedan heard a noise behind him. It was a Roman general, dressed in full armor. Afraid of what it might mean, Aedan turned and greeted him.

"I heard you were open again," the general said, "my horse went lame and I'm behind schedule. Do you have any cubiculae available?" With the general were four other men. They all looked official, not the type he could tell to sleep in the courtyard.

"Of course," Aedan said cheerfully, "please come and get warmed up. While Aedan got some ale for the men, Eira and Maeli quickly got the room she had been in ready for the guests. Aedan and Maeli had been planning on using it for their first night together, but paying guests were a gift from the gods.

After getting the guests settled, Aedan took the horses to the stable and took care of them. It was getting late by the time Aedan slowly walked up the stairs to the family home. When he got there Maeli was gone.

"Where's Maeli?" Aedan asked Seren.

"While you were busy," Seren said, "I planned a surprise for you. Go to the slave quarters." The slave quarters was a small room next to the stables. "Go," Seren stood and pushed her brother, "get out of here!"

Aedan walked down the stairs and across the courtyard to the stable. Off to the side was a door that led to the slave quarters, there was some light coming from underneath the door. Aedan pushed the door open and was surprised to see a bed had been set up in the room.

On the bed was Maeli, covered with a blanket, but her bare shoulders made Aedan's heart speed up. He wasn't sure how they had managed all this so quickly, and without him noticing but he didn't really care. In the lamplight Maeli's hair looked like the flames that were igniting in Aedan's heart. He walked over to his wife and kissed her.

Chapter 24

Cador stood at the base of the broch, the small group of captive women glaring at him. He had been named the champion of the battle and offered the first pick of the slaves. He looked over the women and children. He didn't really want a slave, but Lirra had been excited to get one. Having someone to share in the work was important. It also raised his stature in the clan.

Lirra stood by his side, he wished he could just give the task of selecting one to her. He was the man and he must make this decision for the household. There was a girl in the group about a year or two younger than himself. He walked over to her.

"Where is your mother?" Cador asked the girl roughly.

"Dead," the girl said with defiance.

"You will do," Cador said, grabbing her by the wrist and pulling her towards Lirra. "Take her home and find her a place," he said, irritated that he had to do any of this. After Lirra took the girl away, Cador went to the back of the group and stood sullenly while the other men that had proven themselves were given their pick of the women.

"You did well," Talorc said, coming up behind Cador. "I should have known you were a warrior when I looked at you."

"Thank you," Cador said. He watched the man limp off and thought back to the morning before, this is the man that had caused the fear in Lirra's eyes. That look of fear was one of the worst things he had seen, the woman he loved that much had been hurt by the old man.

Cador couldn't get that out of his mind. He had respect for these men who defended their land and the old ways. He didn't understand how they treated people. Fighting each other for cows or worse their wives and children. He wanted to live in the old way but wondered if he really could.

After the slaves were sent to their new homes, the men gathered for a war council. Cador was a champion now and invited to join them. They sat in a circle around the hearth on the top level of the broch. The wooden floor made Cador think of his old home above the kitchen. He took his seat on a stool as the flames of the fire lit up the room.

"Men," Galan said, "after our great victory yesterday, I'm sure we can expect them to come back for their wives." The men laughed and slapped each other on the back.

"We will be ready," one of the men called out.

"That we will!" Galan called back. "We will plan our next raid after the new moon, until then return to your families and keep ready." The men cheered and all went their own ways.

"Cador," Galan said as he was about to leave, "your wealth is increasing, I'm sure you are happy you joined our clan."

"I am," Cador said as he walked out into the daylight. The walk home was cold as the frigid wind blew across the hills. Cador drew his cloak tight across his chest. The smoke filtering through the thatch roof of the roundhouse was a welcome sight, it meant fire and warmth. As he walked through the door he was greeted by Lirra and the strange girl.

The girl was tall and broad shouldered for a girl. She had hair the color of the red soil they had seen while he and Bran had been walking though the Roman controlled territory. She had narrow eyes and thin lips.

"What's your name?" Cador asked as he threw his cloak onto his bed and sat by the fire.

"Riona," the girl said defiantly.

"Riona," Cador said, "have we found her a place to sleep?" Cador looked at Lirra.

"Yes," Lirra said, "she will sleep on the floor here by the wall." The place that she was pointing at looked cold and uncomfortable. He wanted to object, but remembered this was the way of things. He felt for Riona, but he couldn't change anything. Could he? Cador beckoned Lirra outside.

"Lirra," Cador said once they were outside. "I know that I'm not from here, I grew up very differently. My parents always treated slaves well."

"That isn't our way," Lirra said, "slaves are not people we take care of. They take care of us."

"I know," Cador said. "What if she gets sick. She's no good to us dead. We can let her sleep by the fire. Make her be the one that keeps it going." Lirra thought about that, it would be nice not to have to get up in the cold and put more wood on the fire.

"Fine," Lirra said, "she sleeps on the floor by the fire." Cador smiled, he had convinced her of this, he could win her over to his way of thinking. They went back into the roundhouse to find Riona standing in the same place as before.

"You will sleep here," Lirra pointed to a place closer to the fire. "You are to keep the fire going. I will not be cold."

"Yes, miss," Riona said. Lirra took down a pot and poured some water from a jar into the pot. She instructed Riona to get the smoked boar meat that was hanging by the wall. The two women worked together to prepare food, while Cador watched. Lirra had to give some instructions, but the girl knew what to do.

Cador sat back and decided this was all going to work out.

Part III

Enduring Freedom
4 Years Later

"Taran! Get down!" Druscilla called the toddler climbing on the table. Maeli rushed out to the courtyard from the kitchen to see what her son was up to now. He had climbed onto a bench and was trying to grab a lantern that had been placed there. Druscilla had already grabbed the child and ruffled his mop of curly hair.

"Thank you," Maeli said. She took the squirming boy and held him, "you listen to Avia," she told the boy. They had decided that he could call Druscilla the Romani word for grandmother. Eira had gone by the Briton for grandmother, Nain, until her passing last year. The family was changing, but they were still working together.

Maeli put her hand on her stomach, another child would be along in a few months, she wasn't sure how she would keep up. Across the courtyard Seren was bringing linens out of the guest rooms. At least this child would have a cousin to play with, Seren was also expecting her own child.

Aedan was running the caupona now and had moved his wife and child into the room he had shared with his siblings. Druscilla took the smaller room. Owain and Seren had their own roundhouse a short walk from the inn.

The new servant, Eòin came in from the road with a load of straw for the stable. He smiled as he walked by, the load looked almost too big for him. Eòin was their hired hand, he was fifteen, had sandy colored hair and a nose that looked like it had been broken a time to two. He was fond of fistfights but otherwise kept himself out of trouble. Taran waved and giggled at him.

"Now you let Ma get this bread in the oven," Maeli said as she put him on the ground and handed him a wooden spoon. He immediately started using the spoon to hit all the furniture. Maeli finished shaping the loaves of bread and put them into the oven. Out of the corner of her eye, she watched her son walk carefully into the tabiculum.

"Hello, my little warrior," she heard Aedan say as he entered. Aedan often the evenings in the tabiculum to calculate what guests owed. It impressed Maeli that he understood Roman money. She had grown up using barter and trade to get anything. To her exchanging coins seemed an odd way of doing things.

Aedan came out carrying Taran. He was obviously satisfied with the calculations for the day. The caupona was doing well, the trade between Londinium and the frontier had grown keeping them fully occupied with travelers almost every night. He sat with Druscilla holding Taran on his lap.

"Things are going well," Aedan said, handing Druscilla the wax tablet with the calculations etched into it, "I will head to Londinium to buy supplies in a few days." Druscilla looked at the tablet as if she understood what it all meant. Maeli laughed, Druscilla had confessed to her that she was not very good at understanding all the sums.

"Bring back a cook," Maeli said, sitting. "I don't think I'll be able to keep up." She put her hand on her stomach, which was starting to grow. Aedan put his hand on hers and smiled.

"Of course," Aedan said. They had a hard time keeping anyone working in the kitchen. It meant long hours and dealing with demanding guests. Maeli had learned to cook food that satisfied the Roman palate, but it took most of the day to prepare the food.

A few days later Aedan was walking through the marketplace in Londinium. He once more found himself walking past the slave market. In all these years it had remained the same. At least now the memory of seeing Maeli there was not filled with shame. If had not seen her, he would not have her as a wife, Taran or the new baby.

He still averted his eyes as he walked by, not wanting to be involved. He was moving quickly by when he heard the slaver talking about the strong giant he was selling. Aedan glanced at the platform as was shocked to see his brother standing there tied up and exposed to the world.

Aedan stepped into the throng of men trying to bid on this giant who would obviously be a good addition to any household. Aedan had brought a small purse with him, barely enough to buy the supplies he needed. The bids were already higher than he could afford. It would continue to go up. He would not be able to use money to rescue his brother. Then he remembered something his father kept reminding them as they grew up.

"This man is," Aedan had to think for a minute, "Lucious Lupinus Cadoris, citizen of Roma! You are trying to sell these men a lot of trouble." Aedan watched the Britons in the group step back. They didn't want to be ensnared into buying a Roman citizen.

"Have you the proof?" the man at the stand asked.

"He is my brother," Aedan said, "I hold the proof in my home." The man glared at him, unsure of what to do.

"And who are you?" the man asked.

"Gaius Lupinus Aedanius," Aedan said with more confidence than he felt. He looked at his brother for the first time in all of this and saw shame at needing to be rescued. He wanted to finish this quickly for his brother's sake. Another man in the crowd stepped forward. Aedan recognized his face but couldn't think of his name.

"This man is telling the truth," the man said.

"Who are you?" the slave trader asked.

"Publius Cassius Longinus!" the man declared, there was a murmur in the crowd and Aedan realized how he knew thi man. He had been to the caupona a few times. He worked for the governor as an overseer of the Roman businesses in Britannia. He made sure that everyone paid the proper taxes.

"Thank you, sir," Aedan said, moving closer to Publius.

"I have personally seen his papers," Publius said, "he is a citizen in good standing. Release that man now!" The slave trader glared at the Roman official. He untied Cador and returned his tunic to him. Cador dressed quickly, his expression a mixture of anger and shame. As Cador walked to his brother the slave trader called out again.

"He didn't tell me he was Roman!" the trader said, "he cost me three hundred sestertii!" When the bidding had stopped, they had been to two thousand sestertii. Aedan was amazed at the profit made from selling people.

"I'll give you the three hundred," Aedan said. It would leave him without as much to buy supplies, but it was a good way to keep the peace.

"Add another fifty for the inconvenience," the trader countered.

"Take the three hundred," Publius interjected, "or find yourself in front of a magistrate." The trader took the coins from Aedan and scoffed as he walked back to his platform. Cador joined them, looking upset about the whole situation.

"Thank you Publius Cassius," Aedan said softly, "you stay free at the caupona from now on." Publius clapped Aedan on the shoulder.

"The law is the law," Publius said, "always happy to make sure Romani interests are cared for." He turned to Cador, "make sure you let people know you are Romani."

"Yes sir," Cador said politely. As Pluribus walked off, Aedan surprised his brother with a hug.

"I thought you were lost to us!" Aedan said.

"If I hadn't been captured, I still would be," Cador said sullenly.

"Come," Aedan said, "Seren will be so happy to see you!"

Riona swept the hard packed dirt that made up the floor of the roundhouse. Lirra came into the house, holding the hand of Riva. Riva ran over to the fire with a stick she had found and threw it in, giggling as it was engulfed in flames. This was Riva's fourth summer, and her personality was showing through. She had blond hair, but her darker eyes had Lirra sure it would get darker. Freckles swept her small nose that always seemed to be running.

Lirra had just gone to the broch to ask for news of her husband. It had almost been a full moon cycle since he had been captured. When word had come that the Iron Eagle was attacking clans to the south, Galan had decided that they needed to help their brothers. They returned defeated and Cador was not with them.

Galan had been convinced to send a rescue party a few days ago, but they came back to report that he was gone. Lirra sat on her bed and stared at the flames. Riva was playing a little too close to the fire and Riona gently pushed her back. For some reason this enraged Lirra.

"Don't you touch her that way!" Lirra yelled. Riona fell back in fear. Ever since Cador had gone missing, Lirra had become increasingly unreasonable. She understood as she missed Cador as well. Over the years she had grown to admire him. He always treated her well, like she was a member of the family. She also thought he was handsome, with his broad shoulders and muscular chest.

"Sorry," Riona said. She went back to sweeping but kept an eye on Riva. If Riva got hurt, she would also be blamed. Lirra lay down and turned her back on them. This would make it easier for Riona to watch the child. She would likely need to prepare food as Lirra spent all her time mourning her husband.

Riona started to make a lentil stew that Riva liked. Ever since the baby was born, Riona found herself enjoying her time here more. The little one had won her heart the moment she was given the child to hold so Lirra could rest. Some days she imagined that Cador was her husband and Riva was her child.

Lirra finally came back to life when she smelled the food cooking. She quietly came to the cauldron that was hanging over the fire and spooned some of the lentils into a bowl before sitting on the ground and eating. Riona helped Riva eat her food. As they were eating there was a sound from outside. Riona went to see what was happening. Talorc, Lirra's father, was limping up the path to the roundhouse.

"Is she here?" Talorc asked.

"She's inside," Riona said. Talorc shook his head and went inside. Riona knew she should mind her own business, but that was not her way. She went around to the back of the house and leaned close to the wall to listen.

"Galan was not happy with you," Talorc was saying, "the display you made was disgraceful."

"My husband is gone," Lirra replied. "What has he done to help?"

"Don't forget your place girl!" Talorc yelled. "You may think you are so important, the wife of the giant, but you are nothing!" Riona couldn't help but feel sorry for Lirra.

"The clan has failed me!" Lirra yelled back, "I'm left without my husband!"

"Do you think you are the only one?" Talorc replied. "That is the way of life. Men die and women are left alone!" Riona heard Riva start to cry.

"You've upset her!" Lirra shouted. Riona heard the door slam and then could hear Lirra crying. Riona walked back to the front and quietly entered the house. Lirra was holding Riva, both were crying. Riona sat next to Lirra on the floor and put an arm around her. Lirra buried her head into Riona's shoulder and wept. Riva snuggled up into her mother's lap and fell asleep. A minute later Lirra looked at her little girl and gave a small laugh.

"Imagine being able to sleep like that," Lirra said, "not caring that your life is falling apart." Lirra turned to Riona, "thank you," she said.

"You are stronger than he thinks," Riona said, "I know you are." Lirra sniffed and lifted her head a little higher.

"I am stronger than he thinks," Lirra affirmed, "but I am only a woman."

"So was Boudica!" Riona said, "she burned cities to the ground!" Lirra had heard of the warrior that led the revolt against the iron men. She had been defeated, but not before destroying many cities. Galan had been defeated without being able to kill a single men of the Iron army. Lirra put a hand on her sleeping daughter's head.

"Tomorrow, we start the search for my husband!" Lirra said with determination.

Chapter 27

Cador walked through the stable and into the courtyard as the sun rose. When he arrived home yesterday, Seren was excited that he had returned. Aedan did not tell anyone about the shame he had faced being sold as a slave. As far as the rest of the family knew he was here because he wanted to be. Cador acted as if it was just a happy reunion.

When he was informed that his parents were gone, Cador took that opportunity to walk away and spend some time in the stable. The animals didn't know his shame in being captured. His capture hadn't even taken long, he wasn't defeated after a long battle, he had been abandoned.

When Galan had heard the Roman forces were advancing, he called a war council, Cador had advised against marching to fight them. Better to wait until they were closer. They had ignored him and decided to advance on the Roman army. The whole march, Galan acted like he was going to be the one that defeated the Romans. He loved to tell everyone that Boudica had failed because she was a woman, he was a man and would succeed!

When they arrived, the Roman camp was surrounded by guards. The boar clan lined up and started to beat their shields to get the Romans out of their camp to fight. The Romans came and kept coming. When Galan saw the long line of shields he cowered behind the tree line. When the Romans advanced on the trees, Galan called for a full retreat. Never once entering the fight.

The men ran away, Cador turned to run as well but tripped and fell. He landed in a bush and got tangled up in the branches. By the time he was free from the bush he was surrounded by Romans. They captured him easily and stripped him of his weapons, shield and dignity.

It never occurred to Cador to tell them he was Roman; he was able to understand what they were saying but pretended he couldn't. A translator was brought and told him that he was a captive of the Roman Empire and would be sold. Cador understood how all this worked and watched for any opportunity to escape. None came and he was finally bought by his brother. As if being captured wasn't enough.

Aedan had brought him home and celebrated with everyone the return of Cador. For some reason, this added to the shame Cador felt, Aedan acted like it was nothing to have bought his brother and brought him home. Aedan never asked him why he was there, or even where he had been. Seren did ask but all Cador felt he could say was "north." He didn't tell them about Lirra and Riva, he didn't know why but he wanted to keep it a secret.

The kitchen fire was lit and Seren and the girl with the hair like Riona's but brighter, were already preparing bread and cutting cold meat and cheese for the guests. Cador walked over to join them.

"It so nice to have you home again," Seren said again as he sat. Cador just nodded and took some bread and cheese. He had to admit; the cheese they bought from the local market was superior to the cheese Lirra made at home. "Maeli" Seren continued, helping Cador remember her name, "did you know that Cador once stood up to a man who came here to steal the caupona purse?"

"No," Maeli said, she hadn't really heard much about the big man at all. There seemed to be some controversy about him that nobody talked about. Cador was giving his sister a look to indicate he wasn't interested in reliving the past.

"He wasn't much more than thirteen," Seren continued, ignoring the look "and some thieves came in late. He heard them and came down and fought them off before Da could come down."

"It was one man," Cador said humbly, "and he was drunk."

"Da was proud of you," Seren said. Cador got up and went over to the barrels of ale to pour himself a cup. He really didn't feel like talking about this. He heard a noise and turned to see Druscilla coming down carrying Aedan's child. Taran was a handsome child, curly brown hair and dark eyes. He looked a lot like his father.

"He wants his Ma," Druscilla said as she came down. Maeli took her son and went back to work, letting him sit on the table next to her. Aedan was the last to come down, looking tired. Cador had a sudden longing for home; he had complained to his wife how often Riva woke them in the night. He would give anything to have Riva wake him again.

Cador excused himself to go to the stable again. When he was young the stable was a retreat from people. This hadn't changed for him; the stable was quiet and safe. Cador took a brush from a hook by the grain bin and started to brush the horses.

Cador wondered what his wife and daughter were doing at that moment. Lirra was probably getting Riva dressed and brushing her hair. Riva always liked to go with Riona to milk the cows and feed the chickens and goats. Cador would sit and watch his girls get ready for the day, content with the way his life was going.

He had become respected among the clan as one of the fiercest in battle. He eventually learned to enjoy fighting against the other clans. He had managed to pillage cows and goats and become wealthy. When he was offered slaves, he had told them he had enough with Riona, who managed to do the work of two people.

Aedan came into the stables and joined Cador. He grabbed a second brush and started brushing a different horse.

"Never thought of you working in the stable," Cador said.

"We've had to double up jobs," Aedan said.

"What happened to Rian?" Cador asked.

"The Romans took him after the Senator was killed," Aedan said. Cador listened for any judgement in his brother's tone but didn't hear any.

"I'm sorry for all the trouble I caused," Cador said, concentrating on the horsehair as he brushed it.

"It was a long time ago," Aedan said. "I hated you. You ruined everything."

"I don't even know what I was thinking," Cador said.

"Sure, you did," Aedan said. "You don't like the Romans coming here and changing our ways. Da explained it to me, he forgave you and wanted me to forgive you too. It took time but I decided that hating you didn't really do anything to make my life better." Aedan shrugged. Cador took his attention from the horse to his brother.

"I can't believe he's gone," Cador said. "In my mind he's always here."

"He's here in my mind too," Aedan said, "one thing the Romans can't take away, this land has the blood of our ancestors. His blood now runs with that of his father making the land stronger." Cador put the brush aside and put an arm around his brother's shoulders. Aedan hugged Cador in return. They separated and walked back toward the courtyard.

"Where have you been?" Aedan asked again as they walked to the kitchen.

"Living among the Caledonians," Cador answered, "I live with a warrior clan and have a wife and child there." Aedan stopped walking and turned to his brother.

"A wife and child?" Aedan asked, "where are they now?"

"I'm not sure," Cador said, "I've been gone a month. They should be at home; her father might take care of her. He's a very violent man though, I don't like the idea of him having my daughter in his household." Cador inhaled deeply and looked up to the blue sky overhead. He prayed to the gods they were doing alright.

Chapter 28

Riva was tiring quickly, Lirra stopped and picked her up. They had been walking for a while, Lirra had given Riona strict instructions to care for her home and make sure nobody knew she was gone. She didn't trust Riona not to run away, so she brought Riva with her. That was two days ago, and they were making good time heading south to find Cador.

The sun was high, so Lirra decided to stop for a break and eat some food. She found a clearing in the woods and spread her cloak in the ground. Pulling a loaf of bread from her satchel, she broke it and gave some to Riva who ate hungrily. She had still had some cheese and meat but decided to keep that for later. There were some wild berries nearby, so she collected some which made the meal more pleasant.

Riva giggled to herself and she ate the berries playing a little game with them that Lirra didn't understand. What went on in her daughter's head was a mystery half the time. Lirra smiled though, realizing that her daughter was enjoying this trip better than she was. The ground was rough and they had come across some stretches of briars that she hadn't enjoyed. Lirra had decided to stay away from trails so that she didn't run into anyone that knew her.

Riva lay her head down in the grass and closed her eyes. At home, the child avoided naps like it was a punishment. Out here she was so tired she fell asleep easily. Lirra decided it would be best to take a rest herself. Having her daughter may slow her down but it also gave her a reason to stop and take care of her own needs as well. Lirra lay down next to her daughter and closed her eyes.

The sun had gotten low by the time Lirra opened them again. She was angry at herself for wasting time. Sitting up, she was surprised to see a young boy, sitting there staring at her. He had a quizzical look on his face and startled when she sat up. Lirra felt for the knife she had hidden under her tunic.

He was short and very thin, like he hadn't eaten in a long time. His hair was long and tangled in places. His face was dirty and his clothes were threadbare and had holes. Lirra guessed he might have seen ten summers.

"Who are you?" she demanded. The boy looked at her, confused and he hesitated before answering.

"Cyr" was all he could say. He looked like he hadn't seen another person for a long time. He also looked more hungry than dangerous. Lirra released her knife and pulled out a piece of bread. She handed it to the boy   and he devoured it.

"What are you doing here Cyr?" Lirra asked, but the child just stared at the satchel with the food. "Still hungry?" Lirra brought out some cheese and meat and Cyr's face lit up. Riva stirred and looked up at the boy; she smiled at him.

"Hello," Riva said, Cyr looked quizzically at her and then nodded, still eating. He was obviously lost and had not eaten good food in a while.

"Where are you from?" Lirra asked. Cyr stood up and put out his hand. He obviously wanted her to follow him. Lirra gathered her things and took the boy's hand. With Riva holding Lirra's other hand they walked back into the woods. The sun filtered through the leaves giving everything a green hue. Cyr walked confidently through the forest.

After a few minutes of waking, they arrived at the remains of a wooden fence. The wood that still stood was charred, but most of it was down. It led to a clearing where she could see signs of people having lived there. Lirra let go of the boy's hand and walked around.

In the tall grass she could see where roundhouses had stood, some of the floors were still plainly visible, the grass not able to break through the hard packed earth. The cold hearths that were visible made her feel sad. The actual houses had been burned to the ground, obviously some sort of raid had taken place here.

Cyr pulled Lirra through the burnt-out village to a house close to the middle. He let go of her hand and pointed to some tall grass. Lirra walked closer to the grass where he was pointing and moved it to see what he was pointing at. There was a glimpse of white and then she saw two hollow eye sockets. It took a moment to register it was a human skull. Gasping, Lirra recoiled and turned back to Cyr.

"Ma," Cyr said softly. Lirra wondered if this boy had been sitting here with his mother's dead body while it decayed. He was walking over to a rough shelter that was built up next to a part of the house that was still standing. It appeared Cyr had used branches and some of the material left from the walls to build himself a place.

Embers from a small fire nearby glowed red, so he obviously knew how to make fire. Lirra wondered how long he had been here. When she turned to Cyr, he was showing Riva a piece of wood that had knot patterns that resembled a face. He had tied sticks to it to look like arms and legs. Lirra realized he was showing her a toy he had made, and Riva giggled as he made it do a little dance.

"Cyr?" Lirra said, "you need to come home with me." The sun was getting low so Lirra decided that they should spend the night here and head out at first light. She built up a fire using embers to light it. She found a pot lying in the grass and used that to turn some of the smoked meat into a stew.

As she cooked, she watched Riva and Cyr become instant friends. They ran around the burned-out village laughing and making all kinds of noises. Lirra smiled, she wished it was that easy for her to make friends with people.

After they ate the two playmates snuggled up together and fell asleep. Lirra spread her cloak over the two and moved a little closer to the fire. It was warm enough during the day, but the nights got cold. Lirra wondered how long Cyr had been here.

As the sun came up, Lirra realized she had not had much sleep. The ground was hard and it was cold. She started packing up what little she could and then woke the children up. Holding a little hand in each of hers, Lirra started back for home.

She had not abandoned the idea of finding Cador, she would head back out as soon as she could get Cyn settled somewhere. There was a woman in the clan who could not have children. Lirra wondered if she would be willing to raise the boy. Lirra had a plan now. She would take the boy to her and hopefully be out to search for Cador shortly after.

Cyr had a lot more energy than Riva and would walk ahead and then look back and wait for them. He had been rescued after who knows how long at that burned out village, he was excited to be with people again. When Riva started to tire, Cyr would pick her up on his back and carry her. He wasn't much bigger than she was so it was a bit terrifying to watch, but the thought that he would be concerned for her warmed Lirra to the boy.

The whole walk, Riva would talk to the boy and he would just nod or smile. Even if Lirra spoke to him he would give silent answers. Lirra assumed he was not used to talking. He obviously understood them but never spoke back. During the day they walked slowly and, in the evenings, they would set up a shelter to sleep. After three days they were home.

As they approached the roundhouse, Lirra sensed something was wrong. Everything was silent and there was no smell of smoke. She quickened her step, afraid that Riona had taken the opportunity to run.

"Cyr," Lirra said to the boy, "stay here with Riva. I'll be right back." Cyr nodded and took Riva's hand in both of his. He looked like he understood that something bad was going on. Lirra walked to the roundhouse and slowly opened the door.

Inside it was dark and cold, there were not even warm embers on the hearth. Lirra stepped inside and tried to let her eyes adjust to the dark.

She moved and her foot met something soft. It groaned. She bent down to get a closer look, it was Riona. She was laying there unconscious, dried blood had plastered her hair to her head.

Chapter 29

Cador looked over the horse that Aedan had given him. It was a tall horse, almost as tall as he was, with tan hair. Owain and Eòin were helping bring the tanned leather he had bought from the local tannery. They loaded it onto the horse and helped secure it.

Aedan and Cador had come up with a plan to make it easier to get across the frontier and into Caledonia again. He would travel as a trader, the Romans would not question that, especially since he carried a small purse of coins. Bribes were the best way to make it through if the ruse didn't work. It also made it easier once he crossed the northern border to have some goods for barter and trade.

Cador hid a spear among the leather, most men carried swords, but spears might raise the alarm among the Romans. He would barter for a shield once in Caledonia. Before he left, he had one more thing he needed to take care of. Cador walked through the courtyard to the kitchen where Druscilla was cleaning up.

"Druscilla?" Cador said as he entered the kitchen. "Can I talk to you for a minute?" Druscilla wiped her hands and sat with Cador.

"Aedan told me what happened to Titus," Cador said. "It was all my fault, I know an apology seems small, but I want to apologize for my

actions." Druscilla sat for a moment and stared at
Cador. Her gaze seemed to drill deep into him. He
wished she would say something, anything.

"Thank you for apologizing," Druscilla
finally said. She quietly stood and got back to work.
Cador sighed, he had hoped apologizing would
make him feel better, but it didn't. If he had more
time, he might be able to mend his relationship
with Druscilla, but he needed to get home to his
wife and child.

Aedan and Maeli met him back in the stable
with some food in a satchel for the journey. In the
last couple of days, Cador had grown to admire
Maeli, she reminded him of Riona. He had not
liked taking a slave, but Riona was like a daughter
to him now. He missed her as well.

"How did it go?" Maeli asked. She had been
the one to encourage Cador to talk to Druscilla.

"Not well," Cador said, "she may never
really forgive me. It might never happen. I'm not
sure I would forgive anyone responsible for Lirra's
death." Cador shrugged, but his expression told
Maeli that he was torn up inside.

"You focus on getting to your family,"
Maeli said, "you are always welcome here." She
gave him a hug and headed back to the courtyard to
give Aedan a moment alone with his brother.

"She's a good woman," Cador said as Maeli
walked away.

"She is," Aedan said. "I hope to meet Lirra one day." Cador hugged his brother and took the lead rope for the horse and headed out on his journey home.

The road was busy as Cador headed out. He followed the road north. The last time he had gone this way he had avoided the roads, this journey would be faster on the Roman roads. Cador looked out over the surrounding countryside as he travelled. He could see the Roman influence on the buildings and dress of the people walking along.

Ahead of them was a family, two children traveling with their parents. Cador watched as the children lagged and had to be encouraged to keep up. He found it amusing to see the frustration on the father's face as his children obviously were tired of walking.

After a few miles of travel, the family stopped off at a caupona for a rest. Cador didn't know why the family was traveling but considered how much easier the Roman roads and cauponae made travel. He had a few more hours to go before the sun set so he travelled on.

He stopped at a small caupona as the sun set and got himself settled into a cubiculum for the night. He lay in the comfort of the Roman bed thinking about his wife and daughter. They would likely think he was dead, he hoped they would be alright until he got home.

It took a week to get to the frontier of Roman control. Cador approached the legionaries who were standing guard at the end of the cobblestone road. Beyond them was a path carved into the landscape by constant use. There were several men with horses and wagons ahead of him, all heading north for trade. The legionaries were just waving people through without asking any questions. Cador passed the line without needing to use his bribe money.

The money would still be useful, the people who lived this close to Roman control could use the coins for trade. It would still take several days to get to his home, but he felt like he was almost there.

Chapter 30

It had been a day since Lirra left and Riona was enjoying her freedom. She was taking care of the animals and keeping the house clean. She had even dared to sleep in the more comfortable bed. She allowed herself to imagine that she was living in her own house, and her husband Cador was off fighting somewhere.

As she was sweeping the floor there was a light knock on the door. Riona wasn't sure what to do. She had thought up a story to explain why Lirra wasn't here. She decided to answer. Talorc was standing there as she opened the door.

"I'm here to talk to my daughter," Talorc said, "fetch her."

"She's not here," Riona said sternly, trying to shut the door. Talorc pushed through and walked into the house. "She's out getting berries," Riona continued trying to stop the man from coming further:

"I'll wait for her," Talorc said, sitting on the bed. Riona had to think of something else.

"She took some bread," Riona said, "I think she planned to be gone all day." Talorc looked at her with suspicion but stood again and walked out the door.

"Tell her to see me when she returns," Talorc said as he left. Riona shut the door behind

him and breathed a sigh of relief. She didn't trust
that man, there was something about him that
made her feel unsafe around him. For the rest of
the day, Riona hid in the roundhouse, only leaving
to care for the animals.

That night she slept on the floor close to
the fire. She knew if Talorc came back and found
her in the bed he would get angry. She wished that
Cador was here, she always felt safe when he was
here. She lay there and thought about his broad
shoulders and muscular chest. It was difficult to be
in this house with a man that she found so
attractive and not be able to be with him. She could
only look on from a distance.

The next day she was outside when Talorc
returned. He stormed up to the house and
demanded to see his daughter. Riona tried to keep
her expression calm.

"She didn't stop by?" Riona said innocently,
"I told her you wanted to see her."

"Where is she now?" Talorc demanded.

"I don't know," Riona said, "she doesn't
tell me everything." Talorc glared at her, took a
step forward and slapped her face. Riona gasped
and glared at him.

"Don't talk to me like that," Talorc said, "I
will wait here for her!"

"Yes sir," Riona said. She wasn't sure what
he would do when Lirra didn't return, but she

wanted time to prepare. She needed to keep him calm. The day went slowly as Riona attended to her chores around the man who was getting increasingly upset. As she was working, she found a thick stick in the stack of firewood that she placed where she could get to it quickly if she needed it.

The sun set and still no Lirra, which Riona fully expected. Riona brought all the animals in to keep warm and safe. That done, she took a seat on the ground close to her stick. Talorc had spent some time pacing but was back sitting on the bed. He looked over at Riona, who was working hard to avoid his gaze.

"She's not coming back," Talorc said, "what aren't you telling me girl?" Riona slowly put her hand on the stick and stared at the ground.

"I don't know," Riona said, "she doesn't…" before she could finish, Talorc hit the back of her head. Riona came up with the stick and caught the man on the jaw. He fell back a step before raising his fist and punching Riona in the face. She could feel her eye starting to swell almost as soon as he hit her. Riona was enraged and swung her stick, hitting Talorc behind his ear. Talorc hit her so hard her head snapped back and hit the wall behind her.

Everything went bright white and then started to go in circles. Riona couldn't keep her feet under herself and stumbled forward. She tried to swing her stick again but missed. She felt another blow across the back of her neck as she fell. The world went dark.

Riona became aware of the hard floor but couldn't convince her body to get up. The embers on the hearth were glowing bright. She stared at them for a minute and then decided to close her eyes again.

It was cold when she opened her eyes next. She decided she needed a fire and tried to move, but her body didn't want to. She needed to start the fire again. She needed to sleep again.

There were gentle hands on her face. She was being lifted. She was placed in a bed. She slept.

The house was warm when Riona woke up again. She tried to move, but her arms and legs did not want to move. She called out, and Lirra came to her.

"Hello," Lirra said, "how are you feeling?"

"I can't move," Riona answered.

"I have some willow bark for you to drink," Lirra said. She had boiled the bark in water and made a drink. She helped Riona drink the willow bark and then made sure she was back laying down comfortably. Lirra brought another blanket to keep Riona warm. Making a poultice of yarrow and comfrey, she placed it on her neck and wrapped a cloth lightly around it. She then helped Riona adjust herself so that she could look out into the house.

Riona saw Riva playing in the corner with a strange boy. He had tangled hair and dirty clothes.

"That's Cyr," Lirra explained, "he's an orphan I found in the woods."

"Riva likes him," Riona said with a smile.

"She does," Lirra said, "can you tell me what happened to you?"

Riona told the story of trying to keep Talorc from knowing what was going on. She explained that he had been very angry that she hadn't returned and attacked her. Riona didn't say that she had hit him with the stick.

"I'm sorry that happened," Lirra said, "you've done more than I expected."

"Did you find out anything about Cador?" Riona asked.

"No," Lirra replied, "when I found Cyn I turned back for home."

"What happened to his family?" Riona asked. In the moment they had forgotten that they were slave and mistress, right now they were just two women talking over their problems.

"The village was burned down," Lirra said softly. "I think everyone was dead but him."

"Poor guy," Riona said. Lirra nodded.

"I should get him cleaned up," Lirra said, "are you alright?"

"Yes," Riona responded. Lirra went through some of her old clothes and found a small tunic. She called Cyr over and held it up in front of him. It would be long but would fit. Lirra filled a clay bowl with water and put it by the fire to warm up. She helped Cyr remove his old clothes. Riona noticed that he was skin and bones, she wondered how he had survived on his own.

Lirra gently washed Cyr, using the warm water from the bowl. She gently scrubbed him with her hands and made sure he was clean enough. He stood by the fire to dry, looking content to be clean. Finally, Lirra put her small tunic on him. He looked comical in the oversized tunic.

"We need to do something about your hair," Lirra got out the iron knife she kept by the hearth and sat Cyr on the ground. She sat behind him on a stool and straddled him with her legs. She took the knife and carefully cut the hair above most of the tangles. She used a wooden comb to straighten up the rest. By the time she was done he looked pretty good.

Lirra sent him outside to play with Riva and sat next to Riona again. She laid her head on Riona's bed, after a moment Riona could sense that she was quietly weeping. Riona tried to put a comforting hand on her head but could not move it. She wondered if this would be her life now. Sitting in bed unable to move. She felt a tear fall down her cheek as well.

Chapter 31

Cador had traded most of the leather away for food and accommodation, but finally he was close to the broch. When he saw the top of it on the horizon his heartbeat faster. He would shift his path to miss the broch and go straight to his house. He honestly did not want to see Galan; he was so angry with him for leaving him to the Romans. The path to his house felt longer today than it ever had. He could smell the smoke now and hear his cow complain about something. He was close!

As he came up over the crest of a hill, he saw Riva running in the yard with a boy he didn't recognize. They were playing some sort of game, but she saw him and forgot the game immediately.

"Da!" she called running to him. Cador saw Lirra appear in the doorway, looking as beautiful as he had ever seen her. He dropped the horses lead rope and jogged to his daughter. He lifted her high into the air and laughed as she squealed. Lirra was running to him. He put his daughter down and kissed his wife, holding her as tightly as he dared.

"You're alive!" Lirra said through the tears.

"Of course I'm alive," Cador said, holding her out so he could look at the sun shining on her brown hair and her brown eyes. "I love you."

"I love you too," Lirra said. "Come, I have someone for you to meet!" Lirra pulled him over to where the boy was standing. He was wearing an old tunic, and his hair was cropped short. "His name is Cyn," Lirra said, "he's living with us." She didn't leave it for discussion; Cador knew her well enough to know that she wasn't going to change her mind.

"Hello Cyr," Cador said. The boy looked at him for a moment, nodded and then ran off.

"He doesn't talk much," Lirra said. "Is that your horse?" The horse had walked up to Cador and stopped behind him.

"Yes," Cador said, he grabbed the rope and led the horse to the roundhouse. He tied the horse up outside before stepping into his house. The first thing he saw was Riona propped up in a bed. One eye was swollen and she looked tired. He turned to Lirra.

"What happened?" Cador asked.

"My father," Lirra said softly. "I was out and he got angry and beat her." She could see Cador's muscles tense up as she said it. He walked over to Riona.

"Why did he do this to you?" Cador asked.

"I wouldn't tell him where Lirra was," Riona answered. Cador punched the wall behind him and started for the door. "Wait!" Riona called, lifting her hand.

"You moved your hand!" Lirra said. Riona was looking at it in shock.

"I did!" Riona said. She moved her other arm and then her feet.

"The yarrow worked!" Lirra said. Cador looked at both a little confused. "She couldn't move her arms or legs yesterday. Today she's able to move!" Cador was still angry. He shook his head and rushed out the door. Lirra rushed after her.

"Don't kill him!" Lirra called after Cador. She had to admit, a part of her wanted him to kill her father. She didn't feel right thinking it, but he had been so terrible to Riona.

"I won't try to," Cador said as he stormed off. He moved fast along the path to Talorc's house and burst through the door without knocking. Talorc stared at him with an expression of pure shock.

"Thank the gods, you're alive!" Talorc said, opening his arms to Cador. Cador didn't give it a second thought and punched Talorc on the jaw. Talorc fell back and then regained his footing.

"That's for what you did to Riona!" Cador said.

"Who?" Talorc asked. "You mean the slave girl? She's lucky that's all I did! Your wife needs a beating too for how she's been behaving."

"How has she been behaving?" Cador asked.

"Demanding that Galan and the clan rescue you," Talorc said, "forgetting her place." This statement angered Cador and he threw another fist. Talorc fended off this one and got into a better fighting stance.

"Forgetting her place?" Cador asked. "She was trying to be the best wife she could be. Her place is doing what she can for me!" Cador rushed Talorc and caught him under the arms. He lifted him up to his eye level. "She asked me not to kill you. Was that not her place either?"

Talorc's eyes were filled with fear, he made the wise choice and kept his mouth shut. Cador threw him down and he fell onto the floor. Without another word Cador walked out the door.

"Did you kill him?" Lirra asked as he walked back into the house.

"No," Cador said, he sat in front of the fire and held his daughter close. Lirra sat next to him and wrapped her arms around his and lay her head on his shoulder. To his surprise the boy came up and sat on his other side. "Thank you for trying to get Galan to come after me." Cador finally said. Lirra laughed a little.

"Not that you needed it," Lirra said. Cador laughed as well.

"I don't think this clan is a good fit for us," Cador said, "I'm tired of fighting." Lirra looked down at the boy, who had lost his entire family in a raid.

"Me too," she said.

Coming in June 2026 from
D.W. Lewis

Escape

Book III of the Caerwyn Chronicles

The following is a preview of *Escape*…

The warm wind moved the sand around Taran's feet. He adjusted the scarf on his head and pulled it around to cover his mouth the way he had seen the locals do it. This was his second time coming to the big stone city. He remembered the first time he came to Petra, walking down the long canyon floor, tall red rocks towering over him. Then the canyon opened up to the tall columns carved into the rock. It was awe inspiring.

Taran had grown up in Brittania, the son of an innkeeper. His father had taught him how to manage money, he enjoyed calculating costs and earnings. The people he admired most were traders, people who travelled the world and moved goods. For him this involved two things he liked, travel and money.

When he turned seventeen, Taran joined a party of traders and traveled to the Greek islands. He managed to make enough money during the first few years of working with others that he set out on his own. Now at 20 he was leading a small group of traders to pick up spices to take to Londinium. He brought his group into the city and they settled their horses down near a trough of water.

Taran turned to his business partner, a Greek man named Pyrros. Pyrros was an older man with dark hair and a bushy beard. He had a thick nose and dark eyes.

"You said you had a friend here?" Taran asked.

"Yes," Pyrros responded, "he owns a caravanserais near here. It's a little bigger than your caupona I think." Pyrros liked to tease Taran about the small inn his family ran. The Caupona Caureni was small with only three cubicula for guests. It was on a small Roman road that went from Londinium to the northern limits of Roman control, so three rooms were enough.

"Let's see if we can get a comfortable bed for the night," Taran said.

"That would be good," Pyrros said, clapping Taran on the shoulder. They called the other two men in their caravan and walked through the throng of people through another canyon to where the valley opened up and a vast city became visible. Close to one of the canyon walls was the caravanserais they were seeking. A low stone building with small columns around it. Pyrros said it reminded him of Greece; it reminded Taran of the Roman buildings in Londinium.

They passed through a small entryway, which was low enough that Taran had to duck to get through. He was taller than most men, but still shorter than his uncle Cador, whom he had met once in his travels to Caledonia. He had dark hair and eyes, like most of the locals here, but his skin was pale and his nose was straight, so he still stood out. He removed his scarf and let his curly hair fall down to the nape of his neck.

The proprietor of the caravanserais was indeed a friend of Pyrros and gave them rooms at a reasonable price. Taran paid him with Roman coins and got a big smile in return. They were becoming more common here, but most traders hoarded them.

Coming from a nation that didn't have its own currency before the Romans came, he traded mostly in Roman coins. He kept some Greek and Nabatean coins for use with the smaller merchants.

The room he was led to had stone walls and a small opening near the roof for light. There was a small bed, not ornate but functional and a table with a stool. There was a small basin with water for washing the dust off. For Taran this was enough. He closed the door and removed his tunic to shake the dust off. He then washed himself with the water from the basin.

Feeling human again, Taran went to the courtyard where they had food laid out for them. The food in Petra was nothing like at home, even when the Romans visited. The Nabatean people had specific spices they liked to use. The Romans went for anything, the Britons almost no spices. He got some roast meat and bread and sat with Pyrros.

Pyrros was sitting with two local men. He introduced them to Taran, the first was Malik ibn Sahr, and the second was Zandeil ibn Nūr. Malik was a stately looking Nabatean with a long grey beard and distinctive booked nose. Zandeil was younger with a short beard and a straight nose.

"These men have brought oils from Judea to trade," Pyrros said. "They have fine olive oil, the Romans will pay well, I think."

"Good," Taran said, "we need to find out what they want to trade for the oil" Taran had learned Greek and some Aramaic, but Pyrros was fluent as he had traded in these parts for years.

"I am looking for Roman sestertii," Malik said in Latin.

"You speak Latin," Taran said with surprise.

"There seem to be more Romans here every year," Malik said, "only a fool would not learn to barter in their tongue."

"You are obviously no fool," Taran said, "where are you from?" Malik smiled, in his culture business was the last thing you discussed. This young man obviously understood that.

"I'm a traveler," Malik said. "My family have travelled to wherever the water is sweetest for generations."

"Interesting," Taran said, "my people are bound to the land, each generation makes the land richer with their blood."

"But you are here in Raqmu," Malik said with a smile, "what his people have named Petra."

"The rock," Pyrros said with a smile, "a fitting name for this place." Malik nodded.

"Of course," Malik said. "Your people bring the rocks to their cities; we bring our cities to the rock." Pyrros and Taran laughed at his joke.

"How do you attend to your family if you move so much?" Taran asked, he loved learning how other people lived.

"Or family comes with us," Malik explained, "we have tents that we can carry and move from place to place."

"I've seen it," Pyrros said, "they take their whole house with them when they travel. It's something."

"I would like to see that someday," Taran said.

"I like you," Malik said, "come tomorrow. I will send my boy Hagaru, he is learning Latin. He will bring you to our tent. You will sit and eat with me, and we will make a trade." Malik stood and Zandeil followed suit.